In the grand American tradition of Twain & Hemingway, these travel stories by William Eastlake give us a sharply observant, sympathetic, and always humorous look at the definitely-different world of North Africa and Spain. This book should have been published years ago, but then it is never too late for good writing.

—Edward Abbey

WILLIAM EASTLAKE

JACK ARMSTRONG IN TANGIER

and other escapes

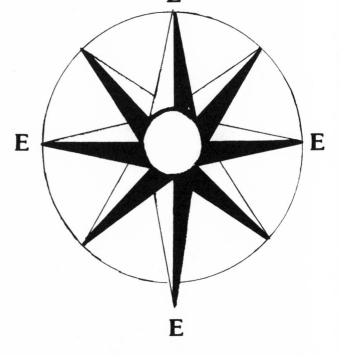

𝕭amberger 𝕭ooks

Flint, Michigan, 1984

Copyright 1966, 1967, 1969, 1970, 1984

by William Eastlake

There's A Camel In My Cocktail appeared in *Harper's*
(4–66)

Jack Armstrong In Tangier, *The Last Frenchman In Fez*, and
The Dancing Boy appeared in *Evergreen Review*
(8–66; 12–67; 12–70)

Dead Man's Guide To Mallorca appeared in *New Mexico Quarterly*
(Winter-Spring 1969)

First Edition
Bamberger Books
P.O. Box 1126
Flint, MI 48502

ISBN 0-917453-00-X (signed ed.)
ISBN 0-917453-01-8 (Hardcover)
ISBN 0-917453-02-6 (Paper)
LCC: 84-71147

IN LOVING MEMORY OF MARTHA

CONTENTS

JACK ARMSTRONG IN TANGIER 1

THERE'S A CAMEL IN MY COCKTAIL 15

THE DANCING BOY 29

THE LAST FRENCHMAN IN FEZ 41

A TALE OF THE ALHAMBRA 55

SOMETHING FOR THE HEART 71

JOHNNY-BEHIND-THE-DEUCE 89

DEAD MAN'S GUIDE TO MALLORCA 99

JACK ARMSTRONG IN TANGIER

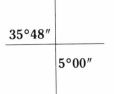

35°48″

5°00″

Jack Armstrong was missing.

The German boy and the English boy were Jack Armstrong's friends and all day and all night they sat at the Café Central across the stage-lighted and Arab-costumed Petit Socco from the Café Tout Va Bien and did not think about the painting they were not going to paint tomorrow or the writing they were not going to write tomorrow.

From Germany, from Berlin, the German boy with the blond beard and blue eyes had got a U.S. Army vehicle down the Berlin Corridor until he got to an ON ramp for the Autobahn where he hitchhiked to Belgium and Luxembourg, arriving in Paris in the rain. It is extremely difficult hitchhiking south from Paris, so you take the cheap third class through Spain. At Algeciras or Gibraltar you get a ferry for Tangier or Ceuta. It is best to go through Ceuta because there is a strict currency control in Morocco and in Ceuta, which is a Spanish base, you can buy cheap *dirhams* on the black market, conceal them in your beard and cross into Morocco a rich man.

There are many other escape routes through from the Iron Curtain Countries. When Yevtushenko coughs and the Iron Curtain sways someone gets through.

The escape route from America to Tangier is direct by Yugoslav freighter. Yugoslavia does not belong to the price-fixing Shipping Commission so it is cheap. Freedom to travel usually means freedom to travel if you have money. That is the intolerance bred by the gentlemen's agreement that seals the American escape route to Tangier except by the Yugoslav Lines.

The German's name was Manfred and he looked like D. H. Lawrence on a good day, excepting that he was more tolerant, less aggressive and much less talented. I say more tolerant because he did not chase small Arab nuisance shoeshine boys away from the small café in the Petit Socco the way Lawrence had at Ajijic. Less aggressive because here he was in Tangier which is the passive hangout. When I say Manfred was less talented I am guessing because the world has never seen anything he wrote. But Manfred was pleasant and relaxed and entirely recovered from his trip from Berlin. He looked across at his English friend, Albert Decker, who

2

was rich enough or foolish enough to have flown BEA to Gibraltar over all the traps that were set all along the escape route for the bearded and the lost. Albert Decker was planning a book of 3,200 pages to be written on an endless roll of paper, actually 472 feet long. It was fed into his typewriter by a Rube Goldberg contraption. He had already bought the paper but, like everyone else, he had not yet begun the book. He had rented a room in almost the exact center of the Kasbah between the Hotel Colon and Maria's which had two lights, yellow and dangling from the ceiling. It had two beds and two chairs and it was large enough for fourteen bedrolls arranged properly, and he paid two *dirhams* a night for it and sold bed space for one half *dirham* a night and so he was getting rich, except that no one paid. He called his room that opened out on an asphalt roof and was conveniently located between Maria's and the Hotel Colon in Downtown Kasbah, the Pad-Hilton.

Albert Decker and Manfred were two of my three friends. The third, an American named Jack Armstrong, was missing. It would have been nice if my friend Jack Armstrong had a more musical and more poetic, a more far-flung name, a name that went with the escape route and the place.

"I can't believe it," I said. "I can't believe that's your name."

"I can't believe that William Eastlake is your name," Jack Armstrong said.

That was ten days ago. Today Jack Armstrong was in jail, in the Tangier jail, then tomorrow his parents were arriving in Tangier from Somerset County, New Jersey, via Air France. That is what the wire that arrived at the Pad-Hilton said.

"Jack Armstrong told me," I said to Albert Decker and Manfred. "He told me to tell his parents that he has gone on a camel-buying trip to Oujda. But I'll think of a more likely story," I said.

"No," Albert Decker of the 3,200 page novel said. He had a gentle, noble, almost feminine, Eighteenth-Century English poet's face. His blond hair was in ringlets and he could have held his own with Shelley and Keats on the Piazza di Spagna. "No," he said. "I think it's a likely story. That's what's wrong with it. A likely story is always suspect. Tell them their son, Jack Armstrong, has become

3

the advisor to the King which means he had to renounce Christianity which means he had to renounce his middle-class background American parents."

"No," Manfred said. "I met an Arab in Tetouan once who told the truth. Why not tell them their son, Jack Armstrong, is in an Arab jail?"

We all thought about this and we thought about the Arab in Tetouan who had told the truth.

"But," I said, "if his parents are coming tomorrow we must cook up something for Jack Armstrong today. I forget what he's in for."

"He's in for two weeks," Manfred said.

"I mean why."

"The Arabs don't have a why," Albert Decker said. "You're used to Anglo-Saxon jurisprudence. In the Arab world they put you in because you're out, and when you ask them why, they give you dark reasons which have nothing to do with the case. It's an indictment of all of humanity, with which you are forced to agree."

"You feel that it's the Arab's heartfelt compassion alone that keeps them from hanging him," Manfred said.

"Let's go to the jail and see him," I said.

The drinks were fifty old *francs* apiece so I gave the waiter two *dirhams* including the tip and we made our way through the press of Arabs in the Petit Socco and up the narrow slit against the flow of Arabs to the Socco Grande. The Kasbah is the inner recess, the final redoubt, the inner Medina. The outer Medina is more open. It is squares where the camels came, now buses, and it is surrounded by a great wall that in most places has fallen down. The Tangier jail is like any jail on Forty-second Street and Broadway, or Selma, Alabama. It is surrounded by soldiers in bright uniforms and the deeper into the recesses of the jail you get the more brilliant the uniforms. When we got to Jack Armstrong the uniforms were blinding.

"Tell me," I said, "exactly when your parents plan to arrive."

"Have you got a cigarette?" Jack said.

"If you've got any ideas—?"

"Did you bring anything to eat?" he said.

4

Manfred handed him a Camel and an Oh Henry. Jack Armstrong put the camel behind his ear and took a bite from the Oh Henry.

"I'd like to read you something I wrote," he said.

Jack Armstrong had the simple, open, honest face of the cowman, the American movie star, the boy your daughter brings home who has won the American Legion Prize. He had a winning smile and a loser's pride, a dimple and a turned-up nose, surrounded by a Tangier jail.

"Let me read this," he said with the Oh Henry in one hand, a Camel behind the ear, the dimple on the far cheek and the manuscript in the other hand. "It's called 'The Night the Midgets Died in Havana.'" Jack Armstrong tossed the Oh Henry wrapper away along with his manuscript and lit his cigarette.

"Tell my parents I'm in the Tangier jail," he said. And then he said, "Sit down."

We all sat down on a wooden bench with Jack Armstrong in the middle.

"You know," he said, blowing out the smoke, "there's nothing like a Tangier jail. Who would have thought," he said, "who at Princeton Prep would have dreamed I'd end up in a Tangier jail?"

"That you would go that far," I said.

"Who are you?" Jack Armstrong said.

"You remember him," Manfred said. "He's our connection. He passes in the outside world. Without him we wouldn't know our way around out there."

"That's right," Albert Decker said. "He lives outside the Medina. People like that can come in handy."

"But he'll steal our stuff," Jack Armstrong said. "If we get a vision he'll be in on it."

"But he's the only one who can talk to your parents."

"No, I can talk to my parents," Jack Armstrong said.

"You can but you won't and he will."

"Is that true?" Jack Armstrong said to me.

"Yes," I said.

"Okay, you're in," Jack Armstrong said.

The jailer came by again to try to sell us some kif, some mari-juana. He had lowered his price.

"Bug off," Jack Armstrong said. The jailer lingered and Jack Armstrong stared him down. The jailer drifted off.

"About my parents," Jack Armstrong said. "My rich father never got in the army. Mother was a brigadier general in the WACs. I remember Mummy in her dress uniforms standing over me with a sword. Pop, rich Pop, put all his hopes in me. He lived for the day when I would be a colonel and outrank her. A colonel doesn't outrank a brigadier general, Mummy said. Actually Mummy didn't have a silver sword. She worked in Washington for the WACs under Oveta Culp Hobby who often came to the house, but poor Pop always saw dangling silver swords and heard the rattle of musketry every time Mummy sneezed. I don't think my father really wanted me to outrank my mother. I think poor Pop figured out very early that the only ploy against such hopeless odds would be for me not to try. To make her look silly in her brigadier general's uniform by not trying. Just Pop and me sitting on the back porch laughing. By going down much further than she could ever go up." Jack Armstrong stopped suddenly and then said quietly, "There's something about a jail in Tangier—."

"We've got to go," I said. "The time's up."

"They'll be staying at the Minzeh Hotel," Jack said. "Give them my love."

The Minzeh is the uptown Pad-Hilton—a thousand dirhams a day and up. It sits in all its fake Arab glory between the Place de France and the United States information library on the *rue d'Ita-lie*. The front door is guarded by two giant Negroes in Arab cos-tume. My friends Albert Decker and Manfred slipped back into the Kasbah because the Negroes at the Minzeh were particular who they let in. They could spot a Kasbah dweller three blocks off. They held giant scimitars at port arms and when I entered they did not cleave me through, dividing me into two equal pieces, but said, "Good morning, sir."

The Charles Armstrongs were ensconced in a nine-room suite overlooking the blood-red houses on the *rue Baclot* and the light cobalt harbor of Tangier where a white Yugoslav boat swung at

6

anchor. They had a dark Moorish servant too, without scimitar, thrown in with the suite. He ushered me through five of the nine rooms and out into the brilliant balcony where the Charles Armstrongs were.

"Scotch or mint tea?" Charles Armstrong said to me.

"I've come about your son, Jack," I said.

"Scotch or mint tea?" Charles Armstrong said.

"Mint tea," I said. "About your son—."

"You said from the lobby you were here about my son," Charles Armstrong said. "I assumed your mission had not changed on the way up."

"Oh boy!" I said.

"Sidney," Charles Armstrong said towards his wife, "this is the messenger from Jack."

"I guess you'd better make that scotch," I said.

Sidney had that female man-face of the aviatrixes in the late '30s. She looked perceptive but insensitive, intelligent but cryptic.

"Scotch for you, Sidney?"

"Roger," she said.

"It was difficult for Sidney to get away," Charles Armstrong said. "But we both enjoyed the trip. I am one of those people," Charles Armstrong said, "that, if it's inevitable, I relax. If we have to make this trip to this hole, wherever it is—."

"Tangier," I said.

"I know that," Charles Armstrong said. "It's just that we can't stay too long. Sidney has commitments."

"Roger. Over and out," Sidney said.

"Two scotches and one tea," Charles Armstrong said to the giant turbanned Moor.

"Three scotches," I said.

"You're not having tea?"

"Not now," I said.

Charles Armstrong gave the order to the Negro, then walked over to the balustrade of the balcony near Sidney and above the white Yugoslav boat.

"I suppose they told you Sidney was a brigadier general?" Charles Armstrong said.

7

"Negative Roger," Sidney said.

"That's Sidney's way of telling me to shut up." Charles Armstrong paused, leaning on the balcony looking back at me. "Did he tell you," he said. "Did he tell you that he could probably go down a lot further than his mother went up?"

"Negative Roger," Sidney said. "Tell me, boy—."

"My name is not boy."

"I'm sorry," Sidney said. "I'm very sorry. I wasn't thinking. Tell me, whatever-your-name-is, where is Jack?"

"In the Tangier jail."

"That's all?" Sidney said. "You're not going to tell us a cock and bull story about his being off on a camel-trading trip or something like that?"

"Not after I saw you," I said.

"My wife is a brigadier general in the American Army and my son is in a jail in Tangier—."

"Knock it off, Charley boy," Sidney said. "It's A-O-K. Scratch it. Now tell me this," she said, not moving her perfect head on the chaise longue. You had the feeling, with her tight hair and horned glasses, that she had on a leather helmet and goggles. "Now hear this," she said. "How did Jack get busted?"

"They accused him of selling kif."

"Marijuana?"

"Yes."

"Is there much money in that?" Charles Armstrong said.

"Negative Roger," Sidney said. "Now hear this. Has he had his court martial yet?"

"He probably won't get a trial," I said. "They can't prove anything. They'll probably let him out in a week."

"Oh Roger!" she said.

"Sidney means Oh God," Charles Armstrong said.

Sidney looked up at the thin, clear pellucid Tangier sky and she let her head swing over to Gibraltar and Spain.

"Someone should teach the Arabs a lesson," she said.

Charles Armstrong began to hop around the balcony. He would take one long jump and hold on that foot, say one word, then take another jump, hold it then a second while he said another word, jumping around the balcony between the red roofs and the pale sky of Tangier and saying, "Sidney. Is. Going. To. Give. The. Arabs. Whatfor."

"Not at all," Sidney said. "The Arabs certainly have a right to arrest Jack if that's what they want to do."

"And if Sidney wants to declare war on the Arabs that's within Sidney's rights too," Charles Armstrong said, making each word separate and definite.

"Over and out, Charley boy," Sidney said.

Sidney took off her glasses, her goggles, and touched them on the chaise longue. "They must want something," Sidney said. "Otherwise why would they be here? I mean, why did they bust Jack?"

"For selling kif," Charles Armstrong said.

"No. That's much too simple," Sidney said. "The Arab is much too complicated, much too insidious, for that."

The Moor brought the three scotches now on a black teak tray. Charles Armstrong reached for the chit but Sidney got it first and signed it.

"Oh hang," Charles Armstrong said.

"No, they're not going to hang Jack," Sidney said. "The Arab is much too clever for that. Is there something else?" she said to the Moor who was poised on one leg with his empty tray. "Give him something, Charles."

Charles drew out a thick wad of many-colored *dirhams* and gave a few of them to the Moor and the Moor quietly folded his leg and left.

"Charles comes from a very rich family. That's why he's so stingy," Sidney said.

"I gave him enough to start a business," Charles Armstrong said. "I gave him ten *dirhams*. How much is that?"

"Two dollars," I said.

"A small Arab business," Charles Armstrong said, and then still talking to me, "Had you intended to tell us Jack was in jail even before Sidney bullied you?"

"Negative Roger," Sidney said. "I never bully anyone. Men have the idea that if women assert themselves simply as human

9

beings that they're tearing men apart and jumping on them. I got ahead in the Army because I only had to compete with men. Actually getting ahead is quite simple, but men are much too complicated for that."

"She was the first woman," Charles Armstrong said, and he said it a little proudly and a little fearfully, "she was the first woman to fly the Atlantic in an airplane with two engines."

"It was simple," Sidney said. "You just point the thing east."

"You see?" Charles Armstrong said. "Wait till the Arabs hear from Sidney."

Now we drank our scotch and watched out at the Yugoslav boat swinging on long anchor in the turquoise harbor below.

"I've got an idea," Charles Armstrong said, leaning over the balcony above the red houses and then looking back at Sidney. "Why don't you, Sidney, get in the Tangier jail disguised as an Arab."

"Oh?" Sidney said.

"Yes," Charles Armstrong said. "Once inside the jail disguised as an Arab man or woman—you could have your choice—."

"Could I?" Sidney said.

"Disguised as an Arab man or woman there's no telling what Moslem pandemonium you could cause."

"Moslem pandemonium," Sidney said.

"I was only throwing spit balls," Charles Armstrong said. "When you got in there I thought you could spirit him away."

"Spirit birit," Sidney Armstrong said.

"I was only trying to be helpful."

"I'm sure you were," Sidney said. "I have decided to go and see the king."

The next day Sidney flew off to Rabat to see the king. Two days later I learned that she was back and then I learned that Jack Armstrong was out of jail and the jailer was in. Everyone who had anything to do with Jack Armstrong's arrest was behind bars. And then I learned that everyone who had proclaimed Jack Armstrong's innocence was given gifts of frankincense and myrrh and small monies, and then I learned that the Armstrongs wanted to see me at the Minzeh, and when I got there Sidney said, "Over and out, Billy boy. Why doesn't our son Jack come and see us?"

"Because you ruined him," I said. "The jailer was a very close friend of his and the jailer's supposed to be out and Jack's supposed to be in. Now you've messed up everything and no one knows who they are except everyone's annoyed with Jack because they figure he had something to do with his parents, with his mother."

"Very little," Charles Armstrong said.

"The Yugoslav boat is threatening never to come back again," I said.

"That's a non sequitur if I ever heard one," Sidney said. "All I did is see the king. He's a numismatist who collects airplanes. I told him where he could get a mint Lockheed Lodestar for peanuts."

"But how did you bring Jack up?"

"I didn't. I saw very little of him as a child."

"I mean how did you bring Jack's name up with the king?"

"Of course I didn't have to. Arab kings realize you don't pay them a visit to get the time of day."

"What's going to happen to the policeman who arrested Jack? If you don't help them Jack will lose face."

"I never liked his face," Sidney said. "But I must see him."

"Then get the jailer out of jail."

"I suppose I could see the local *khedive* or *caliph*," Sidney said. "But I don't want to overcomplicate things and I don't want to do anything again without knowing the local totems and taboos. Why don't you see Jack and find out exactly what he wants?"

I saw Jack at the Café Tout Va Bien in the Petit Socco. When you sit at the Café Tout Va Bien on the east side of the Petit Socco rather than at the Café Central which is on the west side of the Petit Socco it means that you are receiving people.

"That's it, Jack," I said. "She wants to know exactly what you want."

"No one knows exactly what they want," Manfred said.

"And if any of us even knew faintly what we wanted none of us would be in Tangier," Albert Decker said.

11

"Yes, long-term goals," Jack Armstrong said. "Long-term goals are impossible and divisive. And as Jean-Paul Sartre said, if I knew, do you think I'd call myself a philosopher?"

"Your mother wants to know exactly what you want," I said.

Jack Armstrong looked all around the square at the orderly confusion of white-*djellabaed* Arabs in pink turbans and green slippers making their way through the narrow streets, no one pausing to speak.

"I was fond of that jailer too," Jack Armstrong said.

"You'll get over it."

"No, he was a decent fellow," Jack Armstrong said. "And Mummy's orders stopped us right in the middle of a game of chess."

"Couldn't you simply have switched sides and gone on?"

"No. No, they threw me out of jail and they'll never let me back in again," Jack Armstrong said. "Not under any circumstances. Certainly never as a prisoner."

The party broke up leaving Jack Armstrong all by himself.

It was obvious to us all that Jack Armstrong's career in Tangier was ruined, that his only salvation lay in getting out of Morocco for a few weeks, a few months, by which time this incident would be forgotten, hidden in clouds of kif, then he could return. Jack Armstrong agreed to this exile but would not consent to his mother-general's idea of first-class fare home on Air Maroc or TWA.

"We transfer at Madrid," she said.

"The Yugoslav boat," Jack Armstrong said, "is the only classless boat I know outside of the Chelsea Hotel."

"But the Chelsea Hotel," his mother said, "is not a boat."

Jack made this concession and Jack Armstrong's mother-general made the concession to go on the Yugoslav boat, but she insisted on first class. But Jack Armstrong was right about the Yugoslav liner being a classless boat even though he was wrong about the Chelsea Hotel. So two days later, at Ramadan, with Jack not eating anything until the sun struck, with Jack boarding in white gabardine *djellaba* and pointed yellow slippers, they all got on the classless ship and sailed away into a classless sunset.

12

.

"Wait," Manfred said. "Of course he'll come back. But then you never know. His analysis may fail."

"What?"

"Yes," Albert Decker said, all of us still watching the Yugoslav boat steaming with a kind of majestic, forlorn and passive determination toward Gibraltar before it made its turn into the narrow traffic of the straits that would bear it past the Azores and on to the wilds, the jungle of New York.

"Yes," Albert Decker said. "Jack Armstrong will get back there and with his mother's connections he will get a job in the Pentagon or with Merrill Lynch. When he gets back to Essex Falls he will get married, then the conflict will set in between Merrill Lynch and Tangier. He goes to an analyst. If the analysis is a failure he returns to Merrill Lynch and his wife and they live unhappily ever after. In middle age he sends his son, the young, indomitable Jack, to Princeton Prep. The boy revolts and comes to Tangier."

"And if the analysis is successful?"

"If the analysis is successful he kills his wife and only child. I mean, he leaves Merrill Lynch."

"Which is symbolically killing his wife and child," Manfred said.

"Yes," Albert Decker said. "And he himself rejoins us here at the Café Tout Va Bien in the Kasbah in Tangier."

"Which of the two endings do you like?" Manfred asked me.

I said I didn't know and Albert Decker volunteered that he couldn't possibly start his 3,200-page novel until he knew.

"I couldn't possibly make that much investment in time," Albert Decker said, "until I have a resolution."

We all watched out at the Yugoslav boat from the Café Tout Va Bien. The Yugoslav boat, very white against the jonquil sky, was making its wide curving turn westbound, joining three long Greek tankers and the Gran Raffaello. The Yugoslav boat left in the sky a lingering cloud of smoke. The smoke was forming into something that looked like a huge genie, then it became a very clear black smoky question mark. I looked at the others at the Café Tout Va Bien on the Petit Socco to see what they would all make of it, but they had already forgotten all about it and were ordering mint tea and rolling black dream smoke into cigarettes, and where Jack Armstrong always sat there sat another boy, freshly arrived by some escape route.

"My name is—."

"It doesn't make any difference," Manfred said.

"That's right," Albert Decker said. "Here it makes very little difference at all."

THERE'S A CAMEL
IN MY COCKTAIL

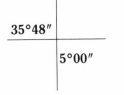

35°48″

5°00″

"Give me the meaning of life in five words," Martha said.

We sat outside the Sidi el Aide in Marrakech, waiting for the king to show up. The king was Hassan the Second and the king was late. The dark Berbers and the bright Bedouins and the small chanting Arabs from the Rif were waiting too, all down the Avenue Moulay el Hassan and the Mohammed Cinque. At the Djemba el Fna the Arabs from the country were excited about the carnival, the circus of dancing *houris*, snake charmers, loud jeweled, gesturing tellers of stories of the feats of Abd el Krim, and the dancing pigeons and the camel that stood on one leg and the Americans with beards.

King Hassan the Second was visiting his winter palace in Marrakech, a splendid fairy jeweled palace surrounded by parks of palms. Bedecked, bejeweled and bewhiskered and betassled, the coal-black Zouave attendants and guards stood in rank, in dark, bright rank, under ribbons of red and bright gold and flags of red and green stars and coronets of wild, gay-blowing flowers, the flag and the heraldry of Morocco. The king was late.

"It looks like the king won't show," Mike said.

"He'll be along in a bit," Albert said. "You American chaps are paying the bill."

Mike gazed into his drink, his crystal ball. "There's a camel in my cocktail," Mike said.

We had met Mike on the boat, on the Italian liner *Leonardo da Vinci*, when we were coming over from the States a long time ago, two months. And we had picked up Albert Decker for the first time here at the Café Sidi el Aide. He was in the Café Sidi el Aide like everyone else waiting for the king. Everyone else included two Canadian girls of eighteen and Martha, my wife. The two Canadian girls had hitchhiked from Vancouver, British Columbia. They both wore tight, stretch-fabric pants, Cossack boots, and bulky knit sweaters, which made them look like shedding camels.

"They're not going to get the king here on time," Mike said. "Why don't we visit the storks?"

"The storks" is what we called the three American boys from Antioch who wore Levi's and smoked hashish and lived on the line between the Marrakech Medina and Kasbah. They lived on the upper floor of a house built before Christ and reached by a very small outer stairwell. The floor had two apartments. The Berbers and the Riffs and the Bedouins and all the other Arab tourists slept on the floor in one apartment, cocooned in their *djellabas*, waiting for the king as they had done for eons, their ancestors, for three thousand years in this identical place.

It was like going into a burning house. The hashish smoke billowed out as we opened the door. It was a heavy deep blue layer upon layer of palpable cloud on cloud so that as you moved through it was like layers of curtains on curtains, and you became enveloped and disappeared. I could see a light somewhere ahead and now I came upon one of the young American gentlemen in Levi's under a hooded robe. He wore a blue turtleneck sweater with a large A on it and was reading a magazine called *Defeat*. Next to this gentleman from Antioch College I could make out the two others in the receding, coiling-toward-the-door smoke. They were holding their hashish pipes, clutching them as though we were a threat. They wore the uniform too, the beard, the sweat shirt, and the Levi's, and they wore the same identical anxious-to-please, retreating, and sorry-to-have-been-born expressions as though the act of smoking hashish bestowed upon them some absolutely blank and inferior status.

"Mike here," I said, "thought you might help him with a camel."

"I dare say," the boy from Antioch said.

"We have been waiting a long time for the king," I said, "and we are getting bored."

"Yes," Albert said. "And rather than do something foolish we decided to ride a camel."

"No," I said. "Mike is going to ride the camel. Mike saw a camel in his crystal ball. He's the one that's got to prove something. He's the cowboy from Colorado. He's the one who can't or won't smoke hashish and is worried about it."

"I dare say," the boy from Antioch said.

"Stop saying that," I said, "and tell me, you've been here a long time, tell me if you have a friend with a camel, know anyone who would rent one."

17

"Oh, I dare say," the boy from Antioch said. And then I realized he must be some kind of mechanical gadget who could say this and nothing more, something a magi had produced and was still surrounded in smoke, something that would disappear when the smoke left. Now the other two beards crept in.

"You want some pot?" they said.

"No," I said. "I don't smoke it. It doesn't bother any of us that we don't smoke it except Mike. That's why he's looking for a camel."

"That makes sense," the beards said. "You've probably come to the only place in the world where that statement would make sense."

"That's why I came here," I lied. "Let me introduce these two Canadian girls who are shedding; Albert here, wearing a British accent. The easel Martha is carrying is a Double-Crostic."

"The meaning of life in five words?" Martha said.

"And as I said," I said, "Mike here is looking for a camel. What's wrong with this man who keeps saying I dare say?" I said.

The gentleman I referred to said in a very low slow rusty voice, "I dare say." Now one of the other bearded gentlemen reached in back of him and pretended to crank him with a quick circular movement. He cranked him fast for about one minute then touched the man's ear as you would touch a button and the man cranked began to say repetitively in a high voice, "I dare say I dare say I dare say I dare say." After two minutes of this there was one final long rundown "Oh – I – dare – say," before he quit.

"Do you want to buy him?" one of the other beards said, the man who had cranked him. "We've sold him many times. That's how we make a living. He keeps coming back."

"I had a horse like that too," Mike said.

I put a few *dirhams* on the low table. "No," I said, "this is how you make a living. It's a pretty good act. As good as the snake charmers, better than the fakirs and the dancing pigeons."

"Oh I dare say," the rusty voice said quietly.

The two Canadian girls stood in the doorway as the smoke fled out and up so that our high stork house at the edge of the Medina at the city wall must have looked like an embattled Kasbah sending signals in smoke to the Rif Mountains of Abd el Krim. The smoke was too much for the real stork and soon we could hear him flap away making a cracking noise like a broken helicopter. The stork should have been used to the smoke now, perhaps selected this spot to enjoy it, probably had a reputation among storks for delinquency, but enough was enough. I could see everyone in the room now. The room was almost a half-circular shape. There was a flimsy straight wall of thick bamboo that separated the boys from Antioch from the Arabs, the Bedouins, and the people from the Rif come to the market and sleeping here for the night. The Arabs must have thought their roommates strange, weird, and exotic creatures, sly and terrible, and from a distant dark country.

"We were at the Sidi el Aide Café," I said, "near the *souks* waiting for the king."

"The king," one of the boys from Antioch said, and they all began to pull on their *djellabas*. Their *djellabas* had fallen down to their hips so that I thought they were swathed in sheets or blankets, but now they pulled them up and I could see that all the boys from Antioch had on hooded *djellabas* just like the other Arabs in back of the bamboo wall.

"This is not nonsense on my part," I said. "I'm here to write about this country, about Morocco, and you can't write something about Morocco unless you've seen a camel close and I don't even feel I've seen Morocco. My closest camel so far was about two hundred yards away, so when Mike saw this camel in his cocktail I thought this would be a good opportunity for me to see one close up. I mean he's got the idea he wants to ride one, so I figured this would be my chance."

"Oh I dare say."

"I guess you can shut up," I said. "I've had enough of that."

"Oh I dare say."

Now I pressed his other ear, the opposite of the one the man had pressed to start him. Both his eyes turned slowly in their sockets and his pupils moved like BBs, then he was absolutely quiet.

19

"Well," one of the other Antioch boys said, knocking out his pipe, "I have got a Bedouin friend down here in the market who travels in camels but he only comes in, he only works on weekends and Shrove Tuesdays."

"Won't he be in to greet the king?"

"Bedouins are against all kings, all authorities. But I have another friend, an Arab who sleeps here on the other side of the screen, a very nice All American Boy Arab who doesn't smoke, who buys camels here at auction and turns them over for a few *dirhams* at his home in Oukaimedem. If you want to ride one and can go a little way with him in the direction of Oukaimedem I think he'd appreciate your breaking it for him. He generally buys wild ones at discounts."

"What do you say, Mike?"

"All right," Mike said.

"Just because I want to write about a camel," I said, "I don't want to push you into anything."

"No, that's all right," Mike said.

When we were all down on the Place Djemba el Fna the boys from Antioch introduced us to a very clean-cut Arab who came from Oukaimedem and dealt in wild camels. He must have spoken five or six languages. I say this because he spoke some English and you don't often sell a camel to an Englishman. For a time in his youth he said he worked for a black-market concession in a *souk* in Tangier when it was an international port. Maybe he learned his English there instead of from some camel-buying Lawrence in Oukaimedem. The clean-cut Arab said his name was Mohammed and he also said you'd go a long way in the Arab countries before you'd find a man who wasn't called Mohammed.

"Now which among you is going to help me with the camel?" Mohammed said.

"I am," Mike said, raising his hand.

"I've been dickering for a racing camel at the airport for three days now. He's a real dog but he can move," Mohammed said.

"At the airport?" I said.

20

"Yes," Mohammed said. "They have phased out all the American air bases in Morocco. Even when the Americans were given permission to build them we saw they had excellent possibilities."

"A place to trade camels?"

"And race them," Mohammed said.

We moved through the Medina; Mohammed knew a shortcut across the Kasbah that brought us out in front of the *souks* at el Mouket. We caught the bus close by at the Harat that took us past the great Souk el Khemis. A *souk* is any market-place. This one went on and on until we got to the edge of Marrakech; then we started through the palm groves that got us out into the flat country, ideal for airfields, bomber bases, and, when the bombers become obsolete, there are always camels. Mohammed had obviously learned his English from the American soldiers at the base.

"I want you to take a good look at this dog," Mohammed said to Mike. "He says it's a sprained tendon but I think it's a small bone in his ankle that may never come right."

"I think I can tell," Mike said.

"You know camels?"

"I know horses," Mike said. "They got the same problems."

"Isn't it a small world," Mohammed said philosophically. "Who'd have thought that at my age I would learn, riding in a bus past the Sidi el Abbes, that a horse was the same as a camel."

"A horse is a camel without the hump," I said.

The three boys from Antioch said nothing. They were all dressed in hooded *djellabas* of different-dyed camel hair. When their hands were back they looked like young martyred Christs. With the visored hoods down-slanting over their foreheads they did not quite look like sly and evil Berbers and Bedouins skulking down from the hills for a holy war; they looked like Antioch boys a long way from home.

We came to a big sign about twelve feet high that read, SAC 149th BOMBER GROUP, and then in large letters, PEACE IS OUR PROFESSION. The bus ran along the fence now that had been stolen.

"The chain-link fence," Mohammed said, "was stolen while the Americans were still here, while they were guarding it. The story

21

goes," Mohammed said, "there was a period of three weeks when the Arabs removed a B59 jet. They carried it away like ants, piece by piece and one morning it was not there."

"Probably not true," I said.

"Yes," Mohammed said. "The story is probably not true, but last week there was a *souk* established in the Medina, the first one, for airplane parts, propellers, engines, all parts."

"A B59 jet doesn't have a propeller."

"That's right," Mohammed said. "It doesn't have anything now."

Now we turned into the main gate of the air base; that is, we turned into the place where the gate had been stolen, and drove out on the five-mile-long runway where the camels were. The place looked as though it had been constructed for camel raising. Piles of camel dung were stacked neatly down the runway as far as you could see. Camels were not the only animals being traded. There were mules, asses, horses, goats, sheep, pigeons, sparrows, and one man had an airplane tire, but the camels dominated the runway and we made straight for them. Mohammed could not locate his Arab from Samarkand with the fast-racing camel with the bad leg.

"But he's knocking off two hundred *dirhams* for the bad leg," Mohammed said. "And with the bad leg he can still go like hell. He's probably in a hangar," Mohammed said, and he disappeared into a huge building alongside the runway which said, PEACE IS OUR MISSION. In a few minutes he came out with the man from Samarkand and the camel. They were watching us carefully as they came up and, I thought, talking about us in Arabic.

"He said he'll trade for five *dirhams* or the three college boys," Mohammed said. "The other deal is three hundred *dirhams* with the three college boys thrown in."

I smiled for Mohammed but the boys from Antioch didn't think it was funny and Martha said, "Don't let him say that even as a joke."

Martha still had her Double-Crostic panel that was shaped like a drawing board or an easel, as though she were going to add up the vast sums of *francs* and *dirhams* and follow the trading with her ball-point pen. "Don't even say that in fun," she said.

The camel was a big evil-looking boy. He looked like an enormous ostrich that has lost even the vestiges of wings but had gained a couple more ostrich legs. One of his legs was hobbled, a rope tied to the foot and pulled up to the same foreleg so that the camel hobbled on three feet. I noticed many of the camels in the runway were hobbled in this fashion.

"It's the only way a wild camel can be handled," Mohammed said. "What about two hundred *dirhams?*" he said to the Samarkander, then he said it in Arabic, and then the Samarkander began to lead his camel back to the camel hangar before Mohammed stopped him by upping the offer in Arabic. The Samarkander looked at the three Antioch boys and Martha said, "Stop that. I told you to stop that." She had the Double-Crostic board over her head now, using it as a shade. "You're doing it again," Martha said. "After all, these boys have parents and they are concerned."

"Do they have parents?" Mike asked. "And why would they be concerned?"

"Don't talk silly," Martha said.

The three boys from Antioch shuffled a little further away from the camel traders. They had on pointed Arab slippers. They were all yellow-colored and conspicious against the white concrete of the runway.

"Would you take a look at his ankle?" Mohammed said to Mike, "and see if you can tell what's wrong?"

Mike touched the camel on the muzzle ever so lightly, so gently, then he moved his hand beneath the great eye of the camel, then in an arc down the neck. When his hand reached the huge shoulder he twisted his body behind the leg of the camel and running his fingers down the leg began to undo the hobble knot expertly. When the camel's foot was free Mike had his whole body into the leg so the camel did not even attempt to move anything. Mike kneaded the tips of his fingers gently along the hock, then into the pastern of the camel. Delicately backwards and forwards Mike moved the tips of his fingers, all the time looking down blankly at the runway, never at the leg of the camel as though it must all be done by feel, that seeing would disturb the delicate sensitive body relationship that Mike had, with his body locked

23

into the leg of the camel and the tips of his fingers probing the small bones and tendons and feeling the reaction.

"You can tell him what you like in Arabic," Mike said. "You can tell him what you like for the trade, but it's not a bone. It's a tendon all right, and probably caused by the hobble. The position of the hobble would stretch the tendon and enlongate it. But it should come back in three or four days okay without the hobble. But tell him what you like."

"Dishonesty is the best policy is an old saying among the Arabs," Mohammed said. "But I always use honesty. It takes them by such surprise they are helpless. There's nothing wrong with the animal," Mohammed told the Samarkander in Arabic. "I will pay you what the animal is worth."

The shock of this statement almost sent the Samarkander down on one knee. He reeled slightly before he recovered, then he must have said, "What is it worth?", then by their expressions Mohammed must have said, "Half of what you asked," and then, while the Samarkander was recovering from that, the two Canadian girls floated into view above a mirage on the other end of the runway. I thought we had lost them on the Place Djemba el Fna, but somehow they had trailed us here. I said before that with their tight elastic pants and loose wool hot sweaters they looked like shedding camels in the zoos of America. I say the zoos of America because, of all the camels I have seen in Morocco and the Sahara, I never saw one shed. They all have perfect tailored camel coats as though out for a stroll on Fifth Avenue. It is only in the zoos that they shed, or it may be that I was in Morocco and the Sahara at the wrong time of year. Certainly the two Canadian girls had arrived at the end of the runway at the wrong time of day. Mohammed and the Samarkander went into a huddle when they saw the girls and began to trade and Martha said, "No, you can't do that." And Mike said from the camel leg he was holding, "They got parents too."

"Yes," Martha said, waving her panel at the camel traders. "Stop them. Don't let them."

"With the three Antioch boys and their *djellabas* and the two Canadian girls in their elastic pants thrown in, no money will change hands," I said.

"Even as a joke," Martha said, "you shouldn't say it."

Now the Arab traders broke out of their huddle and Mohammed came up to Mike and said, "Do you want to try it?"

"Isn't that what we came out here for?" Mike said. "To ride the camel?"

The two Canadian girls came toward us now with the shedding bulk sweaters, through the mirage and the asses and the donkeys and the horses and the used airplane tires and used oxygen masks and bombsights and king-size Coca-Cola bottles till they stood silent near us, silent as always. They were always silent and always following things. I don't remember that they ever said anything.

The camel reached down serenely, not with a quick flustered gesture but with a solemn camel swoop, and took a piece out of one of the Canadian girls. He only got a piece of the bulk camel's hair the girls were shedding. The elastic pants must have frightened the camel. Anyway he settled for a piece of the sweater.

"That's not nice," Mike said to the camel. "We are going for a ride and you've got to learn to behave yourself."

Mike had Mohammed hold the camel's foot in the hobble position while he tied a hackamore around the camel's muzzle with the lead rope, then quickly, deftly, with a lighter-than-air movement, first stepping on Mohammed's back, Mike was on top of the camel before the camel knew he had a rider. The Samarkand camel stood stock still a long moment and then he craned his long neck around, swiveled his bird head, and looked at Mike through long eyelashes — camel eyes as big as footballs, through long eyelashes.

While the Samarkand camel was eyeing Mike, over the Atlas Mountains and far away, but beneath the snow line of the Atlas, you could see a long pall of dust rising like the smog of great American cities. The black dust was rising against the cobalt of the sky and still below the clear vanilla-ice-cream-snow of the Atlas.

"The Berbers and the Riffs," Mohammed said, shading his eyes. "They've come to celebrate the king. To welcome the king."

I guess this is something they have been doing for one thousand, two thousand years, an adventure and a magical rite, coming down the snow-clad Atlas in red and blue and gold on white horses, raising this tornado of dust before you even saw them. But now you could see something. You could see something because they changed the pace, they quickened the pace. They had come in sight of the Mosques of Marrakech. The Mosques of Marrakech, tree-tall and white, emblematic of Allah and the king. All of the Arab horde in a pulsing wave on long following wave approached the American airfield now, PEACE IS OUR PROFESSION, and Mike's camel, still immobile, curious now, waving his trunk of neck, his stalk of neck at his mob of approaching kin. When the flood of Arabs from the hills hit the far end of the runway you could tell from the noise, the screams, the yells, the Holy War, you knew they were going to make a race for it. Never in all of time had Christendom made such a perfect place, an absolute challenge, a smooth and concrete apron spread between the Arabs and their kings. The streaming and screaming windborne Arabs came down upon us so fast and so all at once, there was no time for anyone to move. The trading Arabs and their camels, their asses and their donkeys stood transfixed and rooted, awe-full and amazed. The two Canadian girls, Albert, the dispossessed English boy, the three *djellaba*-caparisoned Antioch boys, the Samarkander and our own Arab, Martha and her own Double-Crostic, all went under in the cloud, all disappeared along with the last vestiges of the American Occupation of the desert. The base was now itself bombed and disappeared. The PEACE IS OUR MISSION, the last Jerry cans, the final spare ailerons, bombsights, obsolete oxygen masks, and goggles were overwhelmed and overcome by the modern barbed Arab steeds, all rushing, all flying, all rushing and mixed and lost in the great wind of the wild Berbers and Riffs going to see and going to welcome their king.

This is what happened. That is what happened to the last American air base in Marrakech, in Morocco. It saved the American taxpayers all that money for the final phasing out, because phasing out is as expensive as phasing in. Some remains of it must still be there beneath the dust. Something for archaeologists to find in a thousand years and wonder what it was. A smooth and hard trading place for camels to the glory of the Arab world, where they traded camels for king-size Coke bottles, used bombs and *djellabas*, and behold! Look here! What is this remnant? From what decline? What fall? From what delinquent and depressed civilization? the archaeologists will ask, this piece of J. C. Penney cloth bearing the word ANTIOCH? And whence these bulky wool sweaters?

"Well," Mike said, back at the Sidi el Aide. "The king did show after all."

"I am looking for an expression," Martha said, "used by the Druids to denote or connote passing of water or time, as it would be translated from Latin into modern Greek in three words."

"Try 'The King is here,'" Mike said.

"Did your friend buy the camel?" I said.

"Oh, the camel," Mike said. "The camel joined the bunch of camels belonging to the king. When he joined the king's herd he became gentle as a lamb. I never saw such a change in a camel. But then, it's my first camel."

"Very good," Albert said. "Quite good. Now that I've seen this I suppose I could go back to England. Here I am, twenty-two years old and I've seen the king. There's not much else, is there?" Albert paused a moment looking out into the pale and amber-lighted square and then he said, with an interrogatory British tilt, "I suppose?"

Mike was staring into his cocktail again, his crystal ball.

"Please don't," I said. "After what we've been through, please not again."

"All right," Mike said. "But I can promise you there's no camel there now."

"Look again," Martha said. "If I can get the answer to life in three words, then I have finished my Double-Crostic."

Mike leaned over and wound up the Antioch boy.

"I dare say," the Antioch Arab said.

THE DANCING BOY

35°48″

5°00″

We were staying at the Minzeh so I met my connection at the Emsallah off *rue de Mexique*. We crossed over to the Mahtura Shasti, then down the Ingleterra to the Grand Socco and the Kasbah. For a connection, the connection was silent. Like most street boys of Tangier he spoke five languages and he was silent now in all of them. How did he know I was not the police? How did he know I was not Beethoven? Beethoven was an easy foreign name for him to remember because there was a street named Beethoven in Tangier, another Bach, another Wagner. Not that the Tangierites are particularly music conscious, because they have another street named Cervantes, and another *rue La Fontaine*, and a *rue Ernest Hemingway*. All this because very recently Tangier was an international city, an international port without customs duty. It prospered wildly under mysterious plots, fraud money, sealed bodies carried through the Medina in the light of day, and princes of the blood living under a *nom de hashish*. But a few years ago Tangier received its liberty from Spain and is no longer a place for the strange — or is it?

Abdullah continued silent. We had a drink at the Tout Va Bien on the Petit Socco, mint tea — tea was all you could get. They had a law, a Muslim law, that covered not only the Kasbah, but all the Medina from the *rue d'Italie* to the *rue de Portugal* — no liquor.

From a slot through the buildings you could see way down past the Gare de Tanger to the bay where none of the great ships came anymore. The world has abandoned Morocco. Everyone stays at home now. The English used to come. The French came, everyone had to come to Tangier somewhere between the ages of nineteen and twenty-six, then they went home and married their neighbor and lived happily ever after, but they had the memory. I do not know where all of the young people of the world go now between the ages of nineteen and twenty-six.

From the Tout Va Bien you could see the Cimetière Musulman which looked grim and, when none of the *djellabaed* traffic was in the way, you could see out through the *rue de la Kasbah* all the way to the Tombeaux Phoeniciens, which was interesting.

"What do you want from me?" the connection said.

"Nothing you do not volunteer," I said. "I am not a journalist. No facts. No lies. I am a writer."

"*Ambiances*," Abdullah said. "*Ambiances*," giving it the French pronunciation. "Would you be interested in my genius?"

"Your what?"

"The Tangier police believe I have a genius."

I did not want to push him or even guide him. This never obtains what I truly want. I must nurture him, tolerate him, accept him, but not push him.

"Would you like some more tea?" I said.

"About the police—. Yes, I'll have more tea. About the police, even when they wanted to become business partners I was so frightened I began to shake. An Arab street boy is supposed to be tough, sly, sophisticated, fearless, but the police always make me shake. Kif, or hashish, sells for twenty-one dollars a kilo in Tangier and one hundred dollars in Paris. It is very simple, a simple business transaction, but I begin to shake. The police want the boys of Morocco to be successful, particularly the children of Tangier. The police know I am a failure, but they will not accept this."

Abdullah took his tea. Abdullah As-Salem As-Sabah sniffed for the mint, then tasted it. The tea of the Kasbah is rank with sugar, so much so that when the tea of the Kasbah cools it crystallizes.

"The police of the Kasbah will not give up," Abdullah said. "Perhaps I could forge documents, become a *contrabandista*, a con man, a blockade runner, a bigamist, a sodomist, a spy, a dipsomaniac, a kleptomaniac, or a nymphomaniac."

"You have to be a woman to be that," I said.

Abdullah sipped his tea before it crystallized. "I use many words that I do not know what they mean," Abdullah said. "To impress myself, but that one I know. Yes, the police want me to become a woman."

"Do you want to explain that?"

"I won't have to," Abdullah said. "I will show you. Come with me tonight to the Dancing Boy."

Albert Decker came up now. He sat down at our table and it began to rain. He ordered tea and the rain began to dilute it, but

31

we sat there until the waiter rolled down the awning with the bright red and green sign, "*Tout Va Bien.*" Albert Decker had a thin blond beard. He looked like a Russian painter from Omsk, but he was an English poet from Sudsbury. He was one of the few English poets between nineteen and twenty-six who still got to Morocco.

"How are things going, Abdullah As-Salem As-Sabah?" Albert Decker said.

"*Tout va bien,*" Abdullah said.

"Have the police found anything for you yet?"

"*Pas encore.*"

"They will," Albert Decker said. "They're determined sons of bitches. Can I read you something that I wrote in jail?"

"No," Abdullah As-Salem As-Sabah said.

"The police arrest us," Albert Decker said, "out of an act of faith. No suspicion, no evidence, pure faith. Jail is really the only place you can write poetry. You can't write poetry in the cafés as my grandfather did in the Paris of the Twenties. The sights here are too distracting. Who can write poetry while being watched by a camel? Who can compete with a whirling dervish? A *houri*? And a cobalt sky? I bet they never had a cobalt sky above the Rotonde in the Twenties. Paris is gray," he said. "That's why we go to jail in Morocco. The police are accommodating. We don't have a Deux Magots, but we have a jail. Can I read you something? A jail with food, lodging, bed, and breakfast all in. Dancing if you tip the warden a few shillings."

"Don't boast," Abdullah said. "Everybody's been in jail."

"I suppose so," Albert Decker said. "Can I read you something?"

The waiter rolled up the awning. The rain had ceased. Abdullah looked up at the Moroccan sky. "No," he said.

"I understand," Albert Decker said. "I don't suppose the police have found anything for you yet, Abdullah As-Salem As-Sabah. Well, I don't suppose they really care. They don't give a farthing really what happens to us poor beggars. I thought I'd have another go at the Muse. You interested, Abby?"

"No," Abdullah said.

"Well," Albert Decker said, rising, "I'll bug off."

No one seemed to object. Not wanting to leave without solicitations to stay, Albert Decker sat down again. He wanted to quit when he was ahead. Albert Decker leaned over toward me above the tea.

"I met Abdullah when he robbed me on the beach. I hitchhiked through Spain with two seventeen-year-old Scottish girls I met in France. I tried to sell them here in Tangier, but the girls sold me. The Arabs wanted my clothes too, stripped me naked here in the Plaza getting them, came to about twenty-three *dirhams*. Not bad, but it was a Bond Street suit, sentimental value, badly worn, the only way to have them. Arabs realize that. Good holes. Clever beggars. So I put on my bathing suit, strolled down the Kasbah to the beach, and slept there. Someone stole my bathing trunks with three pounds ten shillings. Abdullah here waked me, naked there under that cobalt sky, asked me what I wanted. Pants. He got some for me and a policeman came up and demanded his cut. 'We can't have anything illegal going on in Tangier,' the policeman said. 'Honesty is the best policy. The police are your friends.'" Albert Decker felt he was ahead now and got up to leave. "The police will find something for you, Abdullah."

Abdullah As-Salem As-Sabah watched him go. "He is a foreigner," Abdullah said. "Everything to him is comic. He only sees the *comico*. He does not see the tragic because he does not want to. Tomorrow he can get on the boat and leave the country. He is not a victim. He has a passport. No one can do anything to him because he has a passport. So Morocco is a joke. Everything is a joke. With me it cannot be funny. I am getting older, past fifteen."

"Fifteen is not old," I said.

"Fifteen is old for Morocco," Abdullah said. "You are born old in Morocco. All the boys in the Kasbah are old. They speak five languages."

"From the University of Despair," I said.

Abdullah toyed with his spoon. "You were recommended to me by B.," Abdullah said. "You do not behave like B."

"How did B. behave?"

"Like a person," Abdullah said. "Will you be free tonight?"

"Not tonight," I said, "but soon."

33

"But soon," Abdullah said, standing up.

I dropped a pile of *dirhams* on the table knowing Abdullah would distribute it. "Soon," I said, waving myself away.

"But soon," Abdullah As-Salem As-Sabah said, watching me go.

"Was there anything interesting in the Kasbah?" Martha said from her easel on the veranda of the Squiggle Hotel. We called it the Squiggle because this is the way the sign looked in Arabic:

صن زب

"The boy that B. recommended," I said, "has some real genius, but I haven't discovered what yet. When I get back from Fez I will see him again. He seems to know his way around. Did you get anything done?"

"I've been trying to draw those Arabs over there at El Khedive, but they move."

"Send a boy over there with ten *dirhams* asking them not to move," I said. "Are you sure you don't want to go to Fez?"

"Not Fez," Martha said. "I'm still under the weather."

"I could stay and we could see the Phoenician Tombs."

"No, you'd better see Fez," Martha said. "The Phoenician Tombs can wait. I will walk downhill to the station with you and take a Petit Taxi back."

We went down to the train through the Kasbah. In going down to the train or the boat or the buses from the main town in Tangier, it is difficult to avoid the Kasbah without going around where it is extremely steep. There is a wildfire grapevine in the Kasbah and, by the time we got to the Gare Tanger-Fez, there was Abdullah waiting. He did not show up in the waiting room, but outside in the train section where you pay one *dirham* to get in, almost nothing, but enough to keep the poor out. I had called a Petit Taxi for Martha, bought my ticket, and got into the train station. There was Abdullah. "I thought you might want someone to show you Fez."

"Not Fez," I said.

"But you said last night—"

"I mean I can't afford to take you to Fez." Which was the truth, but a blunder. The American is forced into a role in Morocco. Whether he likes the role or not, it is forced on him. In all the poverty of Morocco, the American is a rich man; whether he is a poor American student, a writer, a painter, he is still a rich man in Morocco. His clothing alone is worth the national budget, and when you say you cannot afford a guide to Fez, it is not the truth even though it is true.

The train was late, but that is not true for Morocco either. It was supposed to leave at 8:22 A.M., what everyone in Morocco knows to mean some time in the morning. It was still some time in the morning.

We sat on the wooden bench and watched dry, blue Spain across the Straits.

"Like everyone in Morocco," Abdullah As-Salem As-Sabah said, "I want to go to America, but that is absolutely impossible, so we say we want to go somewhere else. That is impossible too, but it is not crazy. Morocco is the poorest country in the world, but only those of us who speak many languages can even dream about going. The rest are resigned. Do you realize that a passport costs two thousand dollars? I have an American friend who was offered two thousand for his passport in Marrakech. John Siebel from Topeka, Kansas. Do you know him?"

"No."

"Right now I would settle for one dollar—six *dirhams*—to see my dying mother in Ceuta."

"Here is seven *dirhams*," I said, counting it out. "The extra *dirham* is a tip for your mother."

"No one believes the dying mother in Ceuta story," Abdullah said, "so I believe it is not lying. In our small acquaintanceship you would resent it if I asked you directly for five *dirhams* for hunger."

"As long as you don't ask me for two thousand dollars for a passport," I said.

"If I do not find something soon—some way out soon, "Abdullah said, gazing solemnly at the cobalt Straits, "I will end up at the Dancing Boy."

"It's not that bad."

"It is unspeakably bad for me," Abdullah said. "Unbearably bad bad bad bad. Just thinking about it is bad."

"How about another five *dirhams?*" I said.

"No," Abdullah said. "I had planned on five. That is all I need for today."

"When I saw you," I said, "I had planned on giving you ten."

"Thank you, no," Abdullah As-Salem As-Sabah said. "I can only take so much, only the fee, no more than that. To perform the small functions of guiding you for the money is bad enough. When there is only money, something dies. It is dead. There is no longer life. It is dead."

The train was threatening now to leave.

"When you get back," Abdullah called after me as I made my way to the train, "I will take you to the Dancing Boy."

"All right," I said.

"You will not believe it," Abdullah called after me.

The train to Fez passed lonely camels posing on landscaped horizons for the *National Geographic* magazine. It also passed date palms, eucalyptus, and swamps. You do not believe there are swamps on the deserts, but there is a great swamp between Tangier and Rabat. Only the wide, padded foot of the camel can negotiate it, and only the camel tries. The railroad goes around, close to the edge, but around.

I changed trains at Sidi Cassim, got off the train at Fez in a big rain, went with an Arab who knew his way around to the hotel Plicae, and began my tour of Fez when the rain stopped. Two days later I was back in Tangier and Abdullah As-Salem As-Sabah was waiting. How did he know I was arriving on the 10:45? The 10:45 never arrived at 10:45 before, and he did not even know the day I was coming back, but he was there. I do not believe in any form of telepathy, extrasensory perception, but I believe in the Arab.

Abdullah As-Salem As-Sabah was solicitous about my trip to Fez, said he had seen Martha who was well, and the children were a picture of health—"roses in their cheeks."

"But we have no children."

"If you had they would have roses in their cheeks." Abdullah As-Salemm As-Sabah was in fine fettle.

I gave Abdullah a gold coin.

"The Café Tout Va Bien tonight," Abdullah shouted.

"The Café Tout Va Bien tonight," I called back as the Grand Taxi spun off.

At the Tout Va Bien that night Abdullah As-Salem As-Sabah was doleful.

"We don't have to go to the Dancing Boy," I said.

"I must show you my fate," Abdullah said.

"Speaking of fate, when are you going to take Martha and me to the Phoenician Tombs?"

"You would not like them," Abdullah said. "They would bore you." Abdullah looked up. "Do you think your Martha would enjoy the Roman Stadium?"

"I'm sure she would love it," I said. "When was the Roman Stadium built?"

"Last year," Abdullah said. "The nicest view in Morocco," he said, "is another country."

Albert Decker came up now.

"Did you get a passport? Did you find the two thousand dollars? The ten million *dirhams*? Or did you get a job? There are only three jobs in Morocco," Albert Decker said. "The king in Rabat, the mechanic in Tangier, and the dancing boy. Somebody's already got the mechanic job and the king won't be shot for another seven months yet."

"No, I haven't got the passport or the job, but why do you push me?"

"Because you are a genius," Albert Decker said. He looked at Abdullah now. "Why, when a man has as much talent as you do, I can't understand why – ."

"Because the dancing boy," Abdullah As-Salem As-Sabah said, "is dressed like a woman – treated like a woman. You know?"

"But you're in Morocco. We're in Morocco. Right?"

A boy tried to sell us the Gibraltar paper. The wind blew the cloth of the Tout Va Bien over our heads.

"But a man into a woman, even in Morocco – ." Abdullah stared at the paper as though to see some news of this, but blankly. The boy turned away with the paper.

37

"There must be another job," I said.

"No," Abdullah said.

We reached the Dancing Boy by going down all the streets that are on no map. The streets of the Medina are on no map and the inner redoubt of the Kasbah is even unknown to those that dwell there, the people who live near the Dancing Boy. You cannot say it is eleven blocks from the Tout Va Bien because you coast down slippery slits, wind back onto yourself, spiral up and over low rooftops, taste the vileness of sewers and the sweet breath of lurking assassins. The Kasbah is not a city, the road to the Dancing Boy not a street anyone knew, but the whole labyrinth is more like trenches in some war in which the soldiers wear roses in their hats and scream at each other.

Now we were at the Dancing Boy. The music sounded low-keyed religious, and obscene. You entered into a high nimbus cloud of hashish. The players were in a corner on a raised divan so they seemed to be hugging a mountain above the rising cloud below. Hashish smells bittersweet, a kind of green, musky tang, mesmerizing and sweet. Coming through the cloud were the vendors of small boys and girls. They also sold Chiclets and yoyos. One of the vendors had a goat under his elbow.

We sat down in the cloud next to some Sudanese on holiday from Khartoum and three lost-looking pilgrims from Lebanon who smelled of asp.

Decker demanded service by pinching a waiter. The waiter turned out to be God, but he brought us tea anyway. He was a great black man with an enormous white beard. The sail-white *djellaba* he wore bunched up like a dress. He wore thin gold glasses on his wide purple-black face.

"There's no reason God can't be a Black," Albert Decker said. "They're getting all their rights now. This is the kind of place, the kind of cloud, where we would expect to find God."

Abdullah As-Salem As-Sabah was silent, smoking a hashish pipe, but with stateliness, like the great savage who knows where the action is. Abdullah passed me the pipe as though to another voyager. We seemed no longer in Tangier now. We were in the aftercabin of a ship that was lost without a trace. The ship swung

38

gently at anchor. We sat staring at each other over the pipe. You could hear the click click click of something, and a slow grinding screech of something distant, and below that might have been a hawser. Decker moved his hand. His diamonds did not sparkle, they had only a dull greasy sheen this evening in the porthole spot. Out of the sweet dim mist, the sweet bitter soft mist to the left of the Arab orchestra and out on the cloud, danced the dancing boy, dressed like a girl.

The Arab orchestra twanged him or her or it on bravely, twanged on and then reversed itself, and then you realized that's how Arab music goes. The music turns upon itself, swings upward in ever-tightening circles, and then abruptly it is somewhere else, part of the vortex carrying the dancing boy, lifting him and turning him in his gossamer Arabess and Arabesque costume so that he appeared at times only a twirling whirr, something seen off the bowsprit in a cloud, only the cloud was hashish, only the storm was real and violent, only the long tambourines, the thumping drums, the lyre, the lute, the ungodly high screams to Allah and the dancing boy, undreamt of and real.

"Why anyone, why a man would be afraid—"

"Because it's a woman and I am a man.'

"Still," Albert Decker mused through the music, the smoke, the dervish. "Still, it's an Arab culture. They do these things."

"This dancing boy, el Estafa, is going to Mecca next week," Abdullah said. "So that is why they are hiring me."

Soon the spinning boy would be in Mecca. The turning boy in a cloud would be replaced by the one at my side.

We were out of the place, out of the cloud now, and sitting in some alley slit, outside someplace, and someone speaking French with some Riff thrown in. Then Albert Decker moved.

"Well," Albert Decker said, "a boy goes to Mecca and our Abdullah gets a job."

"Or gets killed," I said.

"I don't have anything," Abdullah said. "Not even an enemy."

"I have to go home," I said.

On the balcony of the Squiggle Hotel, Martha said, "We must go to Abdullah's opening."

"I don't think so," I said.

"Then we will leave for Marrakech without seeing Abdullah again?"

"Yes. That is the way he would want it," I said.

But I did see Abdullah again. I saw Abdullah again very dead. Dead.

That's the way it is in Morocco. They die young.

They speak five languages and they die still children.

From hard stuff. A broken needle. The enemy.

Some people don't want to be women. Some do. Some don't. A broken needle . . .

Some don't.

The dancing boy, Abdullah As-Salem As-Sabah was dead.

You would have thought, anyone would think, that the best thing to do is *not* get yourself born in Morocco, not in Tangier, the Medina, the Kasbah. Not get involved with those that do. If you do, forget it. Exactly.

But I can still hear the music, still smell, feel, touch, see Morocco, Tangier, the Medina, the Kasbah, the dancing boy. I guess I always will.

THE LAST FRENCHMAN IN FEZ

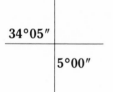

34°05″

5°00″

All Fez is divided into two parts. The neat, ugly, ordered, modern section looks like a middle-class suburb of Paris and is called la Ville Nouvelle and is separated from the exotic Medina, the Arab city, by a careful ten kilometers as though the French had paced it off. The Medina is in the Valley of Kolah, and there is a road that circles it, and you can make the circuit looking down on the disordered, beautiful magenta and mauve, irregular, narrow maze of slit alley streets in fifteen minutes, give or take a few hours for stopping at ancient gates and passing into the soft wilds of the forbidden city. The old city is not forbidden to the French; it is the French who forbade themselves from entering the Medina.

I watched Monsieur Charcot sip a Dubonnet. He tapped the Dubonnet bottle on the bar as though for emphasis and shook his left hand.

"*Nous autres Français, nous sommes foutus.*"

Maybe, I thought to myself, maybe it's because the French colons, the colonials, have such a tenuous hold, such a slipping grip on the French culture, here so far from Paris, that they must not only live in an ugly city exactly ten kilometers from the miracles of the world, but they must also not only not enter the forbidden city but deny it, pretend that the coming of the French with their few tar roads and pathetic steel tracks quickly covering now with sand, would change the face of Africa, and the French must continue to insist on this even now when they are gone.

Monsieur Charcot was one of the last of the French. His father and his father before him and finally Monsieur Charcot himself had owned a vast farm wrested from the sands on the lonely camel track half way between Sidi Hacim and Fez. Three months and twenty-one days, Monsieur Charcot had memorized this, *trois mois et vingt-et-un jours* after the Moroccans had declared their independence, they stole – *Voleurs!* – Monsieur Charcot's farm. Monsieur Charcot blamed de Gaulle equally with King Hassan the Second. De Gaulle had promised that Algiers was France, and was it not fair to assume that Morocco had equal status with Algiers?

"And it did, too," Monsieur Charcot said. "They both went down the drain. *La gouttiére.*"

Whenever Monsieur Charcot talked about France it was strange. He was a Frenchman who had never been to France. Like all colons, whether in the Panama Canal Zone or Morocco, he provoked easily. Although he hated the French, and yes, France too, he loved the Idea. Monsieur Charcot was a *Pied Noir*.

"Yes," Monsieur Charcot said. "When the *Pieds Noirs* helped liberate France in '44 we were charged two *francs* for a glass of water by the French. But let me tell you about my farm."

Each evening Monsieur Charcot finally came to this sentence, "But let me tell you about my farm."

"It was one thousand hectares stolen from the desert. Not the Moroccans, not stolen from them, but stolen from the desert. When they stole it from me it was as green as absinthe. I grew mint, cork oaks, oranges, olives, artichokes, wine grapes, dates and eucalyptus, all as green as absinthe. Now, Monsieur, now it is—. I will take you there tomorrow and you can see."

Tomorrow was a high, deep blue Moroccan sky and a quick-moving Moroccan wind blowing from the Sahara. We got in Monsieur Charcot's 2 CV Citroën. Before we got in Monsieur Charcot insisted that I look underneath the finest car ever built for Morocco.

"Almost a foot clearance," he said. "Now look under here," he said as he opened the hood. It had a two-cylinder air-cooled engine. The front-wheel brakes were in the engine compartment next to the transmission with the driving arms running from the brake to the wheels.

"With this car," Monsieur Charcot said, "you can drive from Algiers to South Africa. Outside of the four-wheel Land Rover it is the only car that can make it. Now get in," he said. The seats were straight canvas chairs that propped you straight up. "Stiff at first," Monsieur Charcot said, starting the engine. "But for a long rough ride there is nothing more comfortable."

We swung quickly out of Fez and soon we were surrounded on either side by great erosions, before we debouched into a flat, slightly undulating plain. The low green and purple mountains in the far right were demarked with a lens of white limestone. Monsieur Charcot drove with a kind of desperate hunger as though he must eat up the distance between Fez and his farm as quickly as he could. He took the corners very fast, cornering close, but the car not skittering as he straightened her out.

"Front-wheel drive," Monsieur Charcot said. "*Traction avant.*" Monsieur Charcot's wide pale face beneath fiery red hair stared out, small and blue-eyed over a steering wheel he frantically mothered.

"The ridge is over there," he said, pointing from the wheel. "That is where we brought the water in. Soon we will come to the bridge. We go under the aqueduct. We worked ten years on this aqueduct. Not since the Romans has anything been done in Morocco. There was almost two thousand years between the Romans and the French. Now Morocco must wait another two thousand years."

"But your kind of Roman progress," I said, "maybe that's not what the Arab wants."

"Oh, that's what he wants," Monsieur Charcot said from the wheel. "It's what he wants if he can get others to do it for him. Not that I minded building the aqueducts. It was a pleasure, a challenge," he said, and then he said, "Oh, my God," and he jammed on the brakes.

"What's happened?" I said.

"Look. Over the road," he said pathetically slumped over the wheel, only holding on now to the wheel, no longer the master. "Look. The bridge over the road," he said. "The aqueduct for the water. It's gone."

"Where would they take it?" I said.

"That's a mystery," Monsieur Charcot said. "The Roman structures are all gone too. What the Arab did with them who knows. Maybe he wants to remove all trace of the conquerer – of a superior culture," Monsieur Charcot corrected himself.

"Who says superior?" I said.

"*C'est vrai, c'est vrai.* True, true, true," Monsieur Charcot said folding his white hands over the wheel. "But anyway my aqueduct is gone. It was built where the Romans built one. Now the farm will dry up and blow away. I spent many Sundays," Monsieur Charcot said, still slumped over the wheel, "I spent many Sundays tracing out the Roman engineering works, the bridges and the roads and the hydraulic works. You have to dig way down to find them. The Arab removed all that shows." Monsieur Charcot started the car again and we proceeded. Now we entered a realm of greenery over a slight rise. The flat land went on in all directions, blooming with mint and olives, oranges like flowers, and lemons like jewels.

"Soon it will all return to sand," Monsieur Charcot said, and then he said, "But I did not come to Africa to work for someone else, like a peasant."

"Why do you say that?" I said.

"They offered me a job," he said. "Working my own land. For them," he said. "For them! Ha ha ha!" It was not a low derogatory laugh but a high insane lamentation. "I did not come to work for the Arab like a peasant," he said.

Now he stopped the car amidst a sea of mint and we got out, and Monsieur Charcot wandered awhile in the mint as though seeing it for the first and last time, and now he got down on his knees and lifted a handful of the red soil and in the other hand he took a sprig of mint and tasted it.

"It must be harvested in four days," he said. "But I did not come to Morocco to work the soil for them like a peasant."

"We've established that," I said.

"Come. I will show you what they do," Monsieur Charcot said, and we got back into the Citroën again. "I will show you how they treat machinery," he said.

We drove up a side road flying in red dust down two columns of eucalyptus trees.

"I planted these for the charcoal," Monsieur Charcot said. "There were no trees in North Africa until the French came and planted these. Now it is quite an industry. The only fuel the Arabs have. Now that we are gone they will be cold again."

"You mean they don't know how to grow a tree?" I said.

"It's not that," Monsieur Charcot said. "It's that when they cut one down they forget to replace it."

Now we came to an asphalt ramp on which all the farming machinery in the world was stashed for rusting. Most of the equipment, the balers, harvesters, and plows were American, big yellow Caterpillars, red and black John Deeres, once-white Fordsons, now seeming to have lost the power of mobility; static and inert, they had begun to flake.

"But why?" I said.

"They've gone back to the oxen," Monsieur Charcot said. "The camel and the horse. Something they understand. I still own this equipment. They let me keep it. But for what? Who would buy it in Morocco now? And there's an export tax and a special foreigner's export tax on top of that. It was very generous of them to let me keep it."

Monsieur Charcot surveyed all his iron worthless wealth as though appraising objects of a lost and fallen civilization made of fool's gold and hammered into an obsolete art.

Between a grove of flowering almond and beds of artichokes sprawled like cactus, came a camel and a horse pulling a plow, the Arab behind seeming not to direct them, but a sheeted bundle risen in the wake of the furrow.

"The Arab learned a thousand years ago," Monsieur Charcot said, "that a camel cannot pull a plow by itself, that is, he's too smart, he *will* not, so some Arab discovered a thousand years ago that paired with a horse, a camel is tractable and will go where the horse is told to go. Since then there has been no progress on the Arab farm," Monsieur Charcot said.

"Listen," I said. "If I'm going to make sense out of this I'll have to get some facts and figures. How many Frenchmen were in Morocco? How much land did they own? How much was expropriated?"

"Facts and figures," Monsieur Charcot said. "Come here in another two months and you'll have all the facts and figures you need. When this is all covered with sand, when it all goes back to the desert it was. That will be the end of the French."

Going back to Fez in a bumping two-cylinder Citroën, Monsieur Charcot kept insisting, "Imagine their effrontery! What gall! What idiocy! Do they think I'm crazy? They offer me a job working on my own land." Monsieur Charcot touched me on the knee. "The Arabs believe I am crazy."

"I do not know what the Arabs believe."

Walking back to my hotel in the Medina I passed the venerable white mosque and I knew the Arabs believed in that, and I passed down the slitted streets into a plaza, shattering water and light above fountains of gold mosaic like altars in monument to life and light and the human spirit, and I knew the Arab believed in beauty. I passed their white-swathed women coiffed in white linen *djellabas* with orange and yellow and silver masks, and again I knew the Arab believed in grace, and the Palais Jamais Hotel was the monument to wonder, with space for gardens and trees and more fountains and courtyards within greater courtyards of mosaic and alabaster and jade and I knew the Arab believed in magic for travelers too.

I had made an appointment to see Monsieur Charcot tomorrow, to eat in his favorite restaurant and drink the only good wine in Fez. But the farm he loved was gone, he was a destroyed and lonely man, and I would not keep the appointment. I had learned all I wanted to learn about the French colon, about the rise and fall of the French Empire at a distance, its facts and figures. Close up it is something fair and just for the Moroccans, and it only takes a piece from the French farmer's heart, a man who had never seen France, whose father, like himself, was born here and hoped to die in the dirt he loved.

A group of Moroccans was standing around a pulsing, pluming fountain on the terrace below. Tomorrow, next year, next month, now that the French have gone, they will be standing more independent, more proud, more self-assured, thinner, more hungry. But you can't have it every way, I thought, and you misunderstand Monsieur Charcot very much, very deeply, if you believe you can take his land, then offer him a job as a peasant. As Monsieur Charcot says, he is not insane.

The following burning yellow day, the sun an almost amber insistence rising against the great white mosque, I took a guide to the Kasbah. You always promise yourself that you will see this Medina or this Kasbah without a guide this time, but then, going down the slope of the hanging gardens, you see a fragile, pinch-faced boy you cannot quite turn away, or you proceed until you get caught and lost in some rootlike tangle of Kasbah maze, and you take the first offer to get you out. The boy I took said he would show me for nothing because he liked – Germans? French? English?

"No. American," I said.

From the Medina we entered the Kasbah through Bab bou Jeloum and saw, felt, the presence of the Medersa bou Inania, an awesome example of Merinide art, then by the Rue Tala through the Babouches Souks where the Arab slippers are made, that pointed, silver and gold and blue and gold footwear of the houris. Men's slippers are made only in yellow and white, but a brilliant yellow and a dazzling white. Now my boy guide pulled me into the Fondouk Tretaouni, a crazy carved platform of cedar wood about thirteen century. I wanted to stop and see all the details but my guide was in a hurry to get to the ninth-century Karaouine Mosque, the largest mosque in the world. If we can't make it better in Fez we can make it bigger. You could see into the prayer hall with its thousands of light columns, but a Christian infidel cannot enter. The Jew and the Christian can only stare across at the Karaouine University which is not only the oldest university in the world, not only where they invented our present system of numbers, the wheel, anticipated Einstein, Sigmund Freud, Charles Darwin, but insist on it.

"C'est vrai. It's true," my boy guide said in English, French, and German as he pulled me towards the Cheritine Medersa trying to complete his tour in twenty-one minutes flat, but from the rise here I wanted to look out on the Kasbah Filala.

"But you haven't completed the tour, sir."

"I see someone down there I recognize."

"But you got to complete the tour, sir."

"That Frenchman over there," I said, "sitting in the Sidi Jahr sidewalk café, the one arguing with the Arabs. Have you seen him before?"

"You've got to complete the tour," the guide insisted.

"Then you never saw him before?" I said.

The guide stopped pulling now and looked over at the Sidi Jahr sidewalk café where the Frenchman with mint tea was arguing with the Arabs who also had hidden behind equally tall glasses of mint tea. There is no liquor sold in the Arab quarter. It is opposed by their religion. Nevertheless, in spite of the mint tea in front of him, Monsieur Charcot was drunk.

"I have never seen him in the Medina before," my boy guide said. "But he used to come to the gate of Bab ou Jaloud to hire workers. He's a farmer."

"A farmer who lost his farm," I said.

"Morocco for the Moroccans," the boy chanted as though repeating something.

"What's left of it," I said.

"You don't have to be with the idea," the boy said. "You should not be with the idea that the Arabs cannot be farmers. After all, we invented the system of numbers."

"And the wheel," I said.

The boy laughed.

"But nevertheless," the guide said. I thought "nevertheless" was a pretty complicated word for a fourteen-year-old boy to use in a foreign language but that is one of the amazing things of Morocco, the street boys who can use so many of the words, and so much of the grammar of five different languages. It makes you feel inept and stupid struggling with French or Spanish, and none of us bothers to learn one word of Arabic.

"Nevertheless," the boy said, "now that the French are gone Morocco will not again go back to the desert, be covered with sand."

Monsieur Charcot arguing at the Sidi Jahr with the three Arabs at his mint tea table got up now and began arguing with the Arab world, telling them all in colon French that they were miserable and incompetent thieves, that if their Allah had any sense of justice—Monsieur Charcot was certain that Allah did—Allah would bring down the revenge of the heavens on the Arabs who were not only incompetent and thieves now, but also ungrateful for all the French had done.

All the Arabs took this sitting down at their mint tea. Most of them must have understood it, and all of them would not be provoked. After all, tomorrow Monsieur Charcot would be thrown out of the country and the least they could do after taking

49

his farm was to listen to his final words, to his farewell address at the Sidi Jahr. I felt now he might be working up to the stage of insults, the Holy War and the chaos and stampedes that followed. I asked my boy guide how much I owed him.

"What you wish, sir. What you will."

"I wish five *dirhams*," I said, passing a note to him emblazoned with a John Deere diesel harvester bringing in the sheaves. On the other side was a picture of the king.

"But," the boy said, returning it, "it is five *dirhams* to the *souks* alone, to the Jondouk it is two *dirhams* more, then one more if you cross the footbridge into the Filala. Then we went by the Palais de Sultan, that is two *dirhams*—. But give me what you will."

"All right," I said. "I will ten *dirhams*," passing him another tractor and king.

"But ten *dirhams* would not ordinarily get you to the Medersa," the boy said.

"Ordinarily it would get me to New York," I said. "Now I wish and I will you good-by."

The boy disappeared in a cloud of Arab dust to find another American to give him what he willed, the boy wished.

Monsieur Charcot was raising his hand for silence. Not that there wasn't already a great silence at the Café Sidi Jahr, so great you could hear a fez drop. It was the awful silence of embarrassment and shame, an Arab silence for the infidel who was drunk and in their home, Monsieur Charcot who had come into the Medina, into the Arab quarter, now for the first time in his life. Now that he was leaving, he had arrived.

"I apologize," Monsieur Charcot said, "for being born. I apologize for bringing water into the desert. I apologize for making Morocco bloom."

The Arabs who spoke French looked at each other from mint tea table to mint tea table with knowledgeable and wise and patient nodding of their heads. Well, anyway, he was the last Frenchman. This would be the final speech. They all seemed to realize it was a small price for inheriting their country.

"*Au revoir*," Monsieur Charcot said, raising his glass of mint tea. "*Adieu*," he said, touching it up against the light of the Arab world. Now the glass of crushed mint began to sway. Monsieur Charcot seemed to be balancing it on the tips of his fingers.

"*Cochons*. Pigs," he said.

A movement, a sway, a perceptible movement ran through the densely packed, robed and hooded Arabs. Monsieur Charcot rescued himself, saved himself from being torn to pieces by the Arab crowd which instantly becomes a mob. Monsieur Charcot saved himself by dropping dead. His descent, his fall into a heap of western clothes and colon Panama hat was so abrupt it left the glass of mint tea still aloft, still hanging in the air. Then it came down in a sudden shower, final benediction, asperging him, a holy water of mint over the body of Monsieur Charcot. The Arabs hesitated and turned their hoods to each other. Allah was just. They had witnessed it. Allah be praised.

I picked up Monsieur Charcot and carried him through the Medina and out of the Sahfid Gate, his body like a newborn camel, all legs, touching against the narrow slit alleys until I got him into a horse carriage, a line of which always waited outside the gate. The carriage was roofless so I used my fez to shield Monsieur Charcot's head from the Moroccan sun. I had a fez. Most foreigners buy something of a beautiful Arab accouterment, a pair of slippers or a silver belt, a *djellaba* or a *cuirass*, something to remind them they have been here. Only Monsieur Charcot who had lived there all of his life here had nothing. As the black Arab steed coasted us at a high steady trot those ten kilometers from the old Fez to the new, from the past to the awful future, I said it's because he's afraid of them, or it's because he thinks he's better. And I knew that wasn't right either. I knew that was too simple too, and I said it's what this country does to all of us. It overwhelms you, makes you feel inadequate. The rest of us make concessions but Monsieur Charcot who had to live a life here could afford to give nothing without soon giving all. After all, a man has to have some identity, to leave some mark that he was here, some sign, some talisman, even that he was embattled, defeated, and overcome.

The concierge at Monsieur Charcot's hotel helped me get him, still sprawling like a young camel, upstairs and on the bed. I sent the concierge down for some mineral water and loosened Monsieur

Charcot's collar, took off his tie. And what in God's name would an Arab think those uncomfortable things were used for? I thought, dangling the tie. Probably to hang ourselves with.

"Well," Monsieur Charcot said weakly, "that was my farewell address, but I do not intend to leave."

"Not go home?"

"You know how they treat a *Pied Noir* in France."

"Well," I said, "anything would be better for you than Morocco."

"Morocco is my home," Monsieur Charcot said weakly.

I made Monsieur Charcot drink some of the mineral water, holding his head and holding the glass to his pale lips. I let his head go back on the pillow and put my glass down.

"My home," Monsieur Charcot said.

"But you have no farm."

"But it is they who will have no farm if they don't give it back," Monsieur Charcot said.

"But how long will that take?"

"Who knows?"

"Yes," I said. "Who knows. And how will you live in the meantime?"

"Oh, that is simple," Monsieur Charcot said. "When I saw you in the Medina today you gave me an idea. Now it is my secret."

"You really believe," I said, "that you will get your land back?"

"Of course. Don't you?"

"In the Arab world I don't know what to believe," I said.

The next day I left for Oujda by way of El Hajeb, Meknes, and Taza. I did not get back to Fez for four days. I was scheduled to get the six o'clock train for Tangier that would connect with the boat ferry for Gibraltar. Before I left Fez I was curious to find out what happened to Monsieur Charcot's farm, but I couldn't even find Monsieur Charcot. I had decided to give up the whole idea and spend a few hours in the Kasbah before getting the train, when I noticed the sand was blowing. It had been blowing steadily from early morning, but now it had increased to where it was a fine curtain that veiled the white houses and the mosques and even made the blues and reds discreet. I got in a taxi and gave the driver directions to take me to the Charcot farm, but when I got but a few miles out to the Oujda turnoff the curtain of sand was coming in so dark and heavy I had to turn back. The Medina walls would protect the Kasbah and the few hours I had left in the Arab world. I would be protected from the weather for a last look.

I had lunch in the Medina in the Dar Saada just outside the Kasbah. After lunch I lit a cigarette outside the Dar Saada and looked up at the hill, at the green hills of Africa. And they are, too, at this time of year in Morocco. The near hill was covered with irregular, ancient buildings and I wondered—.

"That is the Hill el Kolla you are watching, *Monsieur*. The buildings are fourteenth-century Merinide tombs. To the left the dark colorations are olive trees, going down to the Bab Guissa."

I turned to the man in the *djellaba* alongside me.

"But you said you were going home," I said.

"But I am on my way home, *Monsieur*. Would you like to tour the Kasbah very cheap?"

"How much?" I said.

"Whatever you wish, *Monsieur*. Whatever you will."

We started towards the Souks and the voice alongside me began: "When the ancient city of Oualili became too small for the many followers of Sultan Oulay Idriss the Second he sought a more favorable site upon which to construct his capital. Then, during the days of Charlemagne, early in the year 808 A.D. he founded Fez."

"But," I said. "How long can you wait?"

A cloud of white sand swirled over the fifteen-foot-thick Medina wall.

"As long as an Arab," my guide, Monsieur Charcot said.

Now we were coming to the Atterine dating from the fourteenth century.

"Notice the beautiful plaster lacework. *Regardez, Monsieur*." The voice was tense now, alive and concerned. "*Regardez* the light alabaster columns. Notice the play of light on the water and the arabesques formed by the amber."

"*Regardez*," my guide overrode me. "Attention. If you will observe closely, *Monsieur*, you will note the work of the Arab is ingenious, an art to be rediscovered. It seems like a gossamer blown on the wind from another world. *Ecoutez, Monsieur.*"

I realized now my guide had stopped in front of me.

"You cannot beat an Arab, *Monsieur.*" And then he released me by stepping aside and we walked together through the Bab bou Jelout, the entrance to the Kasbah. "And so," he said secretly as though confiding in the darkness, in the shadow of the Moorish gate to another cloaked Berber or Bedouin, "so, *Monsieur*, you join them."

I got my train on time and the train even accomplished the heroic and unknown feat in northern Morocco of making the connection for the ferry to Gibraltar. From the ferry I could see the purple of Tangier and behind Tangier, the Rif and then the Atlas Mountains, all miniature and beholden to the mighty Anti-Atlas, its peaks and giant shoulders heavy with snow. You could see the sand dust drifting in long pennanted shrouds, and somewhere beneath and distant, the farm of Monsieur Charcot. Somewhere in the tangled web, the slitted alleys of Fez, Monsieur Charcot himself pleading patiently but with a kind of adamancy too, Berber-like and Bedouin, "As you wish, *Monsieur*. As you will."

A TALE OF THE ALHAMBRA

37°10″

3°35″

La Señora, our landlady at Torre de Benagalbon, told us that her son Tino, who wanted to be an American, had found a body that looked like an Arab on the beach near our house. Early one morning Tino had gone down to the beach to hit the ball with the bat *como los Americanos*, and he had actually hit the ball the first swing and the ball had rolled down the beach and against the body of the dead Arab that had washed up at ebb tide. The Guardia Civil never discovered who the body had been, what soul it was that the body belonged to.

The Guardia Civil in this southernmost part of Spain, two of them who camped all night on the beach, building small fires and watching for men who run in *contrabando*, the nightwatching Guardia Civil had swooped down on Tino at his first cry with their wide-wing capes streaming behind them like Batmen as they circled the body. Although it was never discovered who the body was, the *Señora* told us her son, Tino, had been very popular as the boy who discovered the body, until quite recently when everyone began to forget. Now Tino had nothing except his American comic books, *Super Hombre* and *El Capitan Marvel*, and his passion to become an American.

"I warn you," Martha said, "don't take the boy to Granada."

"I said if we go to Granada we will have to take Tino because I promised."

"Then break your promise."

"It's not so much breaking a promise to Tino," I said. "It's breaking an American promise. I can't do that."

"One day he will find out that Americans are human beings," Martha said.

"But he won't find out from me," I said. "We'd better take him to Granada if we go to Granada."

"I must see the Alhambra," Martha said.

"Twain said the Alhambra is a fraud."

"Mark Twain said that one hundred years ago," Martha said. So that was that, and the Alhambra had been improving all the time.

Tino's ball hit the window. "He wants to let us know how much he's here," I said, "and how much of an American he is. How much he wants to go to Granada."

"All right, if we have to," Martha said.

Granada and the famed Alhambra is 136 kilometers from Torre de Benagalbon over the Sierra Almijara and along the base of the Sierra Nevada, but first we had to get to Malaga where we would catch the Pullmantur bus. There is a very ancient Toonerville Trolley narrow-track railway to Malaga that runs in front of our house. We caught the train at seven o'clock and Tino was with us. Before we got on the train Tino pointed to a low swale on the beach and said, "That's where I found the body."

"That was very smart of you," Martha said.

On the train Tino went into a huddle with us. He told us that on this trip we were to speak no Spanish to him. He was our American son, he said, and although he might not always understand us we were always to speak to him in American.

"Not English?"

"No, American," he said.

The Costa del Sol is a rugged coastline radiating from Malaga west to Gibraltar and from Malaga northeast to Nerja where the caves are, but now we were on the train going in the other direction towards Malaga with Tino, the Super Hombre, who wanted to speak only American and be our son today, to Malaga to catch the Pullmantur bus that would take us all the way to Granada and the magic of the Alhambra.

"You've got to remember," Martha said, "all of the beautiful things that Washington Irving had to say about the Alhambra."

"Irving lived there," I said. "You can't knock the Alhambra when they give you free rent."

"Oh, I've got it," Martha said. "That's why Mark Twain didn't like the Alhambra. Washington Irving had preëmpted it."

Tino shook his head and pretended to understand everything we said in American. The harder he shook his head in affirmation of our American the more the small dark Spaniards who fish for a living were impressed, and that's how we got to the train station in

Malaga and got out and refused the lottery tickets poked at us, Tino still impressing everyone with his American.

In the office of the Pullmantur I paid the man five hundred *pesetas* apiece for our tickets which would include lunch and Tino and the company of other Americans who were beginning to gather in the office now waiting for the bus that began in Torremolinos and would take us to the Alhambra. It turned out that the other Americans waiting in the office for the bus were Greeks with their Greek wives. It also turned out that they were not going to the Alhambra but were waiting for a bus to take them to America, that is, a bus to Algeciras. From there they would take a boat to the promised land. It looked as though we were going to be the only ones on the bus to Granada until three insidious gentlemen came in and sat down in a corner out of the light. I looked closely in the half light at our fellow voyagers.

"Look," I told Martha, "the one on the left dressed in black with the slouch hat and the dark glasses, he is the Grand Inquisitor returning to the Alhambra."

"But why?"

"And the one in the middle in the military uniform with the yellow gold cape, he is the Captain General. And the one in the corner is King Boabdil, the Caliph, the last Caliph of the Alhambra. They were driven out in 1492 which is an easy date to remember because that's when Columbus left for the States as our Greek friends are doing right now. The date the Arabs arrived in Spain is an easy date to remember too. It was 711, which is a crap game."

The Michelin Guide which I had in my coat pocket said the Moors had all promised to return, and that they are doing it now with us on this bus would be perfectly plausible except that I can't figure out what the Grand Inquisitor would be doing in the company of an infidel like the Caliph. "And it's also surprising that Boabdil would have anything to do with the Captain General, the man who drove him out, and the Grand Inquisitor who would burn him if he came back."

"Probably," Martha said, "they have arrived at some kind of a truce for some odd occasion they're having."

"Probably," I said. "But I still can't figure out what they're doing together."

"The fact that they're here at all doesn't surprise you?"

"No," I said. "Everyone wants to come back to Spain."

The Pullmantur wasn't going to get any more business, it was a bad day, so we all got on the bus with the guide and because the engine was in front in a capsule on the right side of the driver we all sat in the rear to get away from the noise and vibration. The guide sat on the right side of the engine with the microphone. We all huddled in the back away from the microphone so that there was this big gap in the enormous bus until you got back to where we were sitting all in a row on the back seat with the Captain General, the Grand Inquisitor and Boabdil. Tino sat on the arm of the seat in front of us staring at us all, waiting for me to speak American so he could say, "Man, that's a kick, you're turning me on. Cool it, man, before I blow my stack." He had learned this phrase perfectly.

I said, "It's going to be a warm day," and Tino said, "Man, that's a kick. You're turning me on. Cool it, man, before I blow my stack."

The Grand Inquisitor, the Captain General and the Arab King looked at each other, startled and quizzical. It hadn't occurred to me that our three voyagers could understand English, then I realized that Tino was speaking something else, something with such childishness and universality it must have been timeless too, Moorish too, from the days when boys threatened each other with lances and scimitars rather than switchblades.

"Did you notice," I told Martha, "how the Captain General, the Grand Inquisitor and the King looked at each other when Tino spoke?"

"Well, be careful that they can't understand you now."

"We should have no secrets from them," I said and I turned to our three mysterious travellers and said, "*Oiga.* I mistook you for three other people. I thought you were the Captain General, the Grand Inquisitor and the King," I said, nodding towards the Arab dressed in flowing costume. "But you are probably innocent.'"

"But we don't know how innocent," the Captain General said. "It is true that I am in the Army and that your Grand Inquisitor is in the Church and that our Arab friend is of royal blood, and we are all going to the Alhambra."

"Returning to the Alhambra?"

"I can tell you," the Captain General said in ancient Spanish. "I suspect that I can tell you that we have been waiting for a long time in Malaga for our Arab friend to get here. We expected him quite a long time ago but he did not arrive till last week."

"Last week in front of our house," I said to the Captain General, "Tino here found a body on the beach. No soul, just the body. Could your Arab friend here be the soul?"

The three dark travellers looked at each other.

"Could that happen in this day and age?" the Captain General said.

"Tell me this," the Grand Inquisitor said, looking deathily at Tino. "You found a body on the beach without a soul? This is a matter that falls in the jurisdiction of the Inquisition. I mean the clergy," the Grand Inquisitor said. "I suppose you would insist that our friend here, King Boabdil as you like to call him, being an infidel, would have no soul, no soul to separate from the body on the beach, being an infidel, but I say we are always hopeful that everyone will return to the true church. Did the body have any smell of fire about it?" he said, placing his cold hand on Tino's knee.

"Cool it, man, cool it," Tino hollered and ran away to the front of the bus where the guide was.

"That's our little *Super Hombre*," I said.

"I told you," the Captain General said to the others. "I told you that in America now they are breeding a very strange race. Something like," he said looking at King Boabdil, "something like the early Moors at the Alhambra. They will conquer the world or destroy it."

"Or save it?" King Boabdil said.

"No," the Grand Inquisitor mused softly, but with a deadly lilt. "Saving is the province of the Church."

"You notice how jealous," the Captain General said, "the clergy is of their perogatives. Why don't you tell your *Super Hombre* to come back. We would like to study him."

60

"Yes," the Grand Inquisitor said. "It is such a strange new faith."

"Such vitality," King Boabdil said. "Such arrogance. Such ambition and drive. I could have used a million."

I tried to motion Tino to come back but he hung up in front, sitting on the motor between the guide and the driver, looking back at us with a fearful look. The three travellers sat imperturbably and passive as we began to climb the steep terrain out of Malaga.

"You shouldn't bother them," Martha said. "And you shouldn't play games with them. You've frightened Tino. Don't play games. I warn you, don't play games."

"It's their game," I said.

You go up and out of Malaga still ascending past the Gibralfaro, a great ruined Arab fortress that once, for many centuries, defended the town and was the rallying point for the whole coast when the Christians threatened. The Gibralfaro commences the long climb into the Villa Nueva, Concepción and the Sierra Almijara which is contiguous to the Sierra Nevada which lies magnificent with snow. Malaga took a long time to disappear. You could see all the way to Africa now too, which lies dim and blue over the top of the steep Rock of Gibraltar. Gibraltar looks quiet and tough, familiar, old-fashioned, tired, British. Before we got to León, Malaga, Gibraltar and Africa disappeared. We were over the top now of the terrible, dry mountain before Casa Bermeja and beginning to make the long, faster, twirling run along the escarpment to Loja. This was the very rich, for Spain, farming country of Andalusia. The fields grew rocks. Some of the fields grew blue rocks the size of a pebble, others grew a special gray rock as big as a fifty-cent piece, and one farm we passed cultivated white granite rocks the size of a dollar bill. They had cultivated these rocks for a thousand years, the Iberians, the Romans, the Goths, the Arabs, and now the Spanish again. In the spring the wheat and the corn would begin to shoot up through the rocks but now they looked like stone farms, rich in rocks. I don't know why each succeeding generation had not bothered to pick them up. The farms were worked with mules and each succeeding civilization had pushed a little farther up the dry rocky mountain slope for cultivation. Up in the high big rocks now they grew olives. Down below the olives they grew the grapes and it was not till they got down to where it was almost flat that they began the corn and the wheat. The cultivations are so large they must be owned by the very rich and worked by the very poor. The rolling, endless, mule-manicured monument to the failure of some revolution.

The Captain General, the Grand Inquisitor and the King, up here in the brightness of the escarpment now and in the full chrome effulgence of the modern bus with the glass roof, looked less like potentates, the Grand Inquisitor less ominous, the Captain General less glittering, the King less regal. They took on more the aspect of the expensive, cheap brilliance of the German bus, but Tino still feared them. He stayed up on his perch on top of the motor looking back at us with the wide, vacant, no-eyed awe of little Orphan Annie. You would expect suddenly a balloon to appear over his head with the inscription, "What are you doing to me?"

Now the three travellers tilted, huddled forward out of the light as though conferring in their secret black art, and they took on their former aspect of the Grand Inquisitor, the King and the Captain General, and the balloon appeared over Tino's head inscribed, "I told you so."

We swayed into the country before Loja, the country of tobacco and almonds. At first you thought you were climbing into the snow of the Sierra Nevadas, but when you got closer you saw it was the waving, scintillant, icy snow-whiteness of almond blossoms; each close-together gnarled candelabra tree bearing a sparkling bouquet festooned, bejeweled and cold white. The dull elephant ears of tobacco grew lower down and were now safely draped on long poles in the tobacco houses. These are the curing houses where they attempt to administer to the bad tobacco of Spain, to cure it of what ails it, but they have great failures—the Bisontes, the Celtas, the Goyas, all those *finos cigarillos* in exquisite packaging still burn and smoke and savor of old underwear. The curing houses are enormous stone pointed piles with huge ventilating holes beneath the eaves. At this stage of the process the tobacco wafts along the Sierra and smells good. It must be something they do to it later that causes the underwear odor. Smoking it in a pipe, it is not too bad and that's the way I manage it.

"A long time ago," the Captain General said in a faint distant voice of remembrance, "before the English came, the tobacco was good."

"So the English are to blame for that too?" I said.

"Yes," the Captain General said with a touch of the ice of the Sierra in his voice. "Yes. History claims that the English rediscovered the Alhambra, that it had been allowed to go to ruin, that it was inhabited by *contrabandistas*, farmyard fowl and goats. That Wellington saw the beauty there and began uncovering, reconstructing it. That is not at all true."

Each time the Captain General made an iceberg pronouncement his two practitioners of the dark sciences slowly nodded their heads in deathly profound agreement excepting sometimes the Arab King just stared out of non-recognition as though he had been away a long time and out of touch.

"Another thing," the Captain General persisted, "is that the French actually blew up two tower walls in the Alhambra when they fled during the Napoleonic invasion. That was the French contribution. Have you seen what Goya painted about the French? The peasants being stood up against the wall and shot. Goya was anti-everything. He was anti-clerical," he said, touching the Grand Inquisitor with a quick eye. "He was anti-aristocracy," he said, touching the King.

"And anti-military," I said, touching the Captain General.

"Not really," the Captain General said, relaxed as though sure of himself now. "Not really. Goya had a compulsion, a love affair, a secret demon that loved violence. He fought it with his mind but he was troubled by his soul. Like most writers he could not resist violence. But Goya was alone. Goya was Goya," the Captain General pronounced. "An original. I knew him well."

We were in the outskirts of Loja now, but the Captain General was not looking out. The Grand Inquisitor was looking inward and the King was bored by the blankness of the close buildings now that we were no longer driving through the country.

"What do you do for a living?" the King asked me.

"I write."

"But what do you do seriously?"

"I write seriously," I said.

"Then tell me a story," the King said.

"I can't think of one," I said.

"Then tell me something about anything," the King said. "You must know something about something."

"The wines of Spain," I said.

"Good," the King said.

"The best wines around are the Marquis de Riscal and the Marquis de Murrieta. If you can get a good year."

"And what's a good year?" the King said.

"Fifty-four. Fifty-five," I said.

"Fifty-four, fifty-five. Have we come so far so soon?"

"All out for hamburgers and Cokes," Tino shouted.

The three dark travellers did not move, but Martha and I got out and joined Tino in the restaurant that overlooked Loja and the hills beyond. We had coffee and brandy. Tino had his Coke and kept repeating in Spanish—he spoke Spanish when no one else was around—Tino kept repeating over his Coke, "I am not going on that bus with them."

"Why not?"

"There's something wrong with them," Tino said.

"They are very impressed with you as an American," I said. "They have been talking about you. They appreciate you."

"What did they say?"

"That you Americans are a strange race, a little frightening and strange."

"That's exactly what I was thinking about them," Tino said.

Tino got back in the bus, even sat halfway down the bus, a few yards closer to the strangers, but he didn't trust them enough yet. Tino didn't think they were safe enough yet to take his eyes off them. As we sailed down the road that swept above and to the right of the gray-red tiled roofs of Loja, Tino kept watching them. We were on the level now, sliding and swaying past the houses of Spain with clothes tatter-worn, over-washed, faded, draped from balcony to balcony, the flags of Spain, emblematic of poverty and defeat. We were nearing Santa Fe now, the place where Isabella chased after Columbus to tell him the deal was on. "Congratulations, Chris," she said, slapping him on the back. "How are you fixed for sails?" Santa Fe is also the place of the Cuesta de las Lágrimas, the Hill of Tears, where the last Arab king took the final look at Granada and the Alhambra. "It is meet that you weep like a woman for something you could not defend as a man," his queen said.

The bus squeezed through the streets of Santa Fe. The Grand Inquisitor was staring at the floor; the Captain General's eyes were straight ahead. The King said quietly, "She was a shrew, a bitch. I'm sorry," the King said, "but I was provoked."

"We will soon be in Granada," Martha said. "These buses are confining. When we walk through the Alhambra we will all feel better."

"It's been a long time," the King said.

"An eternity," the Grand Inquisitor said.

"And it's only a day's march over the Sierras," the Captain General said.

When we got to Granada we sped quickly through the town, up the Calle Reyes Catolicos to the Alhambra. We stopped in front of the Gate of Justice guarded high up by the Arab Hand. We all got out and went through the arch and left behind the Christian country of heavy, dank, Spanish Gothic, oppressive Baroque and ugly Rococco, and entered a light fairy world of feathered filigree, gay marble columns, soaring Moorish arch and alabaster fountain shattered in water, the singing, cool, glory world of the fled Arab, a miracle of art.

We walked through a far country of enchantment, the Hall of the Arab Ambassadors, the soaring, feathery golden arch of the Abencerrages, past the Vermillion Towers, and as we entered the Court of the Lions, the Captain General walked slightly to the fore as though he were in absolute command, followed by the Grand Inquisitor with an attitude and mien of absolute control, then our Boabdil, curious and yet afraid to look, as though, like a genie, it would all disappear in a puff of smoke. Tino was missing.

"I'll have to find him," I said.

I went back to the magic of all the places we had been, but no Tino, and then I remembered, standing in the magnificence of the Abencerrages, that before the Moors had left they had placed an enchantment on the Alhambra, that before they had departed through the Torre de los Siete Suelos, crossing the Rio Xenil and the valley below of the Condel, then looking back, had issued the Ultimo Suspiro del Morro, the Last Sigh of the Moor, then they had placed an enchantment that had captured Tino now, Tino the American, one of the great violators of the secret beauty and spirit of the Alhambra. And then I thought, *perdón, hermano, por el amor de Dios*, excuse me, brother, for God's sake, but Tino is not an American and there has been no spell of enchantment placed upon the Alhambra. All those fabulous stories of the American Superman, the Batman, Captain Marvel, are all just that; there is no *Super Hombre* in that world and no enchantment in this. Tino is around here someplace, maybe hidden in his arrogant intrusion, camouflaged in the lapiz lazuli or the Moorish peristyles. He could be hidden in the open belvederes of the Torres Vermejas, exposed and invisible. But the Super Hombre had melted, disappeared in the enchantment of the Alhambra. But where? God knows, *Señor. Dios sabe.*

Now the Captain General entered beneath the peristyle. Enter the Captain General bearing Tino, towing Tino by a wrist.

"*Por Dios*," I said. "You found him."

"No," the Captain General said. "I caught him. He was darting across the Plaza de los Aljibes going down into the Darro to the gypsy caves. The Gypsies are dangerous. No one has any authority over them. The Gypsies are like Americans."

"Thank you," I said, taking Tino.

"We will see you in the bus," the Captain General said, disappearing in a cloud of smoke—disappearing in dust actually, caused by the tourists' cars.

"Let's go see the Gypsies," Tino said, pulling me.

"All right," I said. "Let's go see the Gypsies."

"He said it was dangerous," Martha said.

66

"But we don't have to fear," I said. "We've got an American with us," I said, touching Tino.

We went down into the valley of the Darro through the Zacatin, a small Kasbah amidst all this Christianity, and we arrived up out of this filth to the Sacromonte where the Gypsies hide. It is a great, barren, dry hill, adjacent to and even dominating the Alhambra, but still within the time-pocked walls. The Gypsies hide in the caves of the Sacromonte until the enemy, the tourist, has ascended such a distance up the Sacromonte that there is no longer any retreat. The tourist is well within the mine fields, the fortress of the Gypsies, the small caves where the Gypsies hide and wait underground until the picket children, the sentries, report the tourist well trapped, then they sally forth and cut off the tourist's escape, then you are surrounded by Gypsies three deep. They offer to tell your fortune, read your palm, read your mind. Then they offer to black your boots, cash your checks, sell you a child. Then you are being pushed, not so much pushed as caught in a flood of people, going down into a dark cave lighted by Coleman lanterns. It is like something occupied by troglodytes, then Visigoths hiding from Romans, Moors from Christians, Christians from Saints, and now these Gypsies hiding from the gallows way down here where no Spanish soldier dare pursue. The men had long, curled, black, graceful hair like women, and the dark women had tight, bright-colored dresses split to the waist with a flounced and ruffled train. The children were all naked, and squeaked in high mouse voices. The adult Gypsies spoke every language there is. They tried German on us first, then French, Italian, Roumanian, before they finally got to English.

"I knew it all the time," a Gypsy said.

"You were just showing off," I said.

The Gypsy was stripped to the waist. He wore tight Levi's, black tennis shoes, a gold ring in one ear and a Kennedy half-dollar dangling from a thin chain from his neck. Behind him the cave walls were hung with gay-colored American license plates—NEW YORK, VISIT THE WORLD'S FAIR was over his head and IDAHO, EAT MORE POTATOES, was alongside his left ear. The whole cave was adazzle of copper pots in the steady flame of the

Coleman. The cave was strewn with heavy and rich rugs of the Orient, so with the pots shining, the license plates glistening and the rugs redolent of warmth, we felt the poverty and the opulence of the very poor.

The Kennedy Gypsy took my wrist, grabbed it in the wet vise of his hand, turned it slowly, pressured it until my palm opened.

"My daughter will read your palm."

There was a silence.

"When you have crossed it with silver," he said.

I could see this was only the beginning. I could also see that there was no way out and we were surrounded four deep now by their eyes, by their small savage Gypsy eyes, all gathering, all sharp points of light in the cold room. It was a mistake of the Kennedy Gypsy, his shining, begreased, marcelled head now just to the left of black and yellow New York, to take my left hand rather than my right. When I hit him he fell exactly where I wanted him to fall, touching Rhode Island with a clink as he came down to tangle with the others as we ran back through all those glinting pots, through all of the fifty states, back there where I knew there was some exit. But we only rushed through a greater darkness now, a blacker, wetter, a Visigoth and troglodyte gloom without a pine torch, a Coleman, only a batlike kind of sonar sounding that kept us going straight all the lung-hurting distance to where there was a spot of light, a spotlight, a way out. When we got there it was only a hole going straight and impossibly up for maybe three hundred feet to a spot of jonquil sky. No exit.

From out the black behind us now one man walked. You could hear his footsteps echo many miles. He was just within the blackness. It must have been one of them, selected from among the many for the honor, the privilege and the prize of doing us in. The man stepped into our jonquil light now. It was the Captain General.

"Did I not tell you something about the Gypsies?" he said to Tino.

But Tino was white and curled and blanched, huddled together into himself, incapable of sound.

"Did I not warn you?" the Captain General repeated.

"You only said that the Gypsies were like Americans," I said. "But coming after the King, the Grand Inquisitor and you, who knows what to believe?"

Going back to Malaga in the Pullmantur bus, Tino continued up front with the guide and driver as far from our trio of fellow travellers as he could get. It got dark quickly and we slept going down the long swooping hills of Andalusia away from Granada. The bus made two stops on the outskirts of Malaga, probably at hotels, but I heard no one get out. At the Pullmantur office, when the interior lights of the bus went on, our three fellow travellers were nowhere.

We caught the seven o'clock on the *ferrocaril* going back to Benagalbon. On the train while we were going through Rincon de la Victoria, Martha said, "Tino's awfully quiet." And then she said, "They were probably just ordinary tourists. That's the problem living with a writer."

We spent two more weeks at the *Señora's* house at Torre de Benagalbon. Tino ceased his consumption of American comic books. The Batman and Captain Marvels had disappeared. Tino was no longer a *Super Hombre*. Tino spoke Spanish again. Tino never found any more bodies on the beach without souls. I told him to keep his nose clean and hit the line hard. I told him that if things got tough to punch his way out. But he didn't listen. Tino was no longer interested in America.

SOMETHING FOR THE HEART

40°24″

3°41″

We met the king in a railway station in Barcelona. It was a wedding cake pile railway station which had been built in the last century and gone down hill. We met the king at the *bocadilla* bar. A *bocadilla* is a kind of sandwich they make in Spain. That is, we met the *Condessa* there and the *Condessa* led us to the king. That is, she led us to his mysteries which is the same thing. Being led to the mysteries of the king is better than the king himself who is actually a shy, diffident man who smokes Chesterfields, and his only snobbery is not using the mails. The *Condessa* had a message from him she was taking to a man in Seville. This is important because we finally ended up bearing that message from the king.

"*Es suyo,*" I said, picking the message up off the floor where she had dropped it near the *bocadillas.*

"My God!" the *Condessa* said in English. "My God! Let me kiss you," and she kissed me on the forehead, holding my head with two hands so I couldn't escape, and then she went over and sat with her luggage. I went back to where brave little Martha was sitting and asked her how she was doing.

"I'm feeling better," she said.

"Did you see that?" I said.

"Yes," she said. "I saw it."

"That lady," I said, "speaks English. Maybe she can tell me how much later the train will be."

"Ask her if it's going to leave this day," Martha said. "Say, '*Donde está el tren? El tren sale está día?*'"

"Jesus, I don't know," the *Condessa* said. "You were speaking Spanish, weren't you? The train will get off when it gets off. Give it another five minutes." She said something quickly to the porter and motioned us to follow him.

The train was the *Talgo,* a light, all-aluminum train made in France. The problem was that the rails were made in Spain, so the train bounced all those three hundred miles to Madrid.

"No, the problem is," the *Condessa* said, "they have not yet welded the tracks. They have two miles of welded tracks outside of Zaragosa. When we get to Zaragosa, notice the feeling you get."

The *Talgo* is an American-type train. It does not have compartments as all European trains do, so you could see everyone. Most of the passengers seemed like Spanish business men. They were all dressed in tight, too-close-fitting clothes with short jackets of poor quality. They all had wine-drenched faces and smoked American cigarettes which are cheaper here than in the States.

It was three o'clock, lunch time in Spain. We said we would take the lunch, and this kept us busy for the next three hours. They erected a silver platform in front of us and the first thing we got was *entreméses surtidos* served with a chilled white wine. The *entreméses* were brought in on almond-shaped plates. *Entreméses* consist of myriad *cosas de interés*, like innocent gambas with blue eyes, two kinds of squid in its own ink, another kind of crayfish with brown eyes which seem belligerent, green caviar and yellow mayonnaise, then some snails that look out at you from their twisted shells with saucy scorn. Now are placed on your plate many things you cannot identify. There was an *objet d'art* about as big as a golf ball and with spines on it, some shellfish with a secret morsel inside. The waiter surrounded this with slices of fish *au vinaigrette*, then built a second defense of camembert and *paté de foie gras* that had been pressed into molds to make it look like people. As he was making this still-life on my plate I was drinking the white wine from Cordova and looking out the window at Cervera. The waiter had finished his creation now and Martha began trading things with me. She gave me a sea animal shaped like a heart. "I've got two of these," she said, and she stole a blue lizard in aspic.

"That's the only one of those I had," I said. "It may be the only one in the world."

She gave me half of it and I put it in my mouth and it tasted like blue lizard in aspic. The *Condessa* said that the only place in the world that the *entreméses* were better than on the *Talgo* was an old place in Madrid that she had discovered.

"It is called the Ritz. I think you would like it," the *Condessa* said.

We insisted that the *Condessa* do the rest of our ordering, and the next thing we got was an orange and blue fish that did not fit on the plate. It looked alive and happy until the waiter opened it up. It was a very delicate sole cooked in Madeira and brazed under

73

a light flame. The waiter had brought an even lighter white wine to go with the sole and it seemed to match the hint of Madeira in the fish.

"A good fit," the Condessa said, looking through the wine. "The Talgo is improving."

But the tracks were getting worse and the train shook and swayed through another course, the omelette, but the wine helped to steady the train and flatten out the roadbed. The omelette was cooked with *fines herbes* garnished with fresh mushrooms and sprinkled with parsley. It was a conservative omelette. The only theatrical touch, the Talgo chef's *coup de theatre*, was to *flambé* it in brandy and top it with an anchovy.

"The chef is getting brave," the Condessa said. "I approve of taking risks. I think now he has gone a bit too far." She clutched her fork in thought, tasted the omelette again and said, "No, he survived this," then said, "I must know his name. I admire courage. Now," the Condessa said, "shall we try his *entrecôte*?" We all thought we were making a daring move when we braced ourselves and said we would.

"Just this once," the Condessa said. "After all, we should give the Talgo a chance. He's a brave man." I think the Condessa meant the chef.

On the *entrecôte* the chef had backed up and decided to play it safe.

"He's probably tired after the omelette," the Condessa said. "After all he's probably suffered great failures. I wonder how old he is. He cooked it in a French sauterne," she said, savoring it on the tip of her tongue. "He would not risk a Spanish wine. There is a chef at the Ritz who risks it every day," the Condessa said. "Such courage. When a man gets older, what can you expect?" The Condessa seemed annoyed, then dismayed, and then finally settled into a *noblesse* resignation at fate and man's getting older.

"Drink all the wine in your glass," the Condessa said abruptly. "That makes the *entrecôte* bearable."

We did as she said as she watched us.

"Now," she said, "the *entrecôte* will be all right." And it was, too.

"Now there is a surprise," the *Condessa* said as the fingerbowls were brought and the *Talgo* gave a lurch and the water showered her knees. None of us knew till this point that she had a dog. It seemed part of the great fur coat she was wearing; it was almost under her arm but on her hip. The Peke came out for the shower of the fingerbowl water, small, repulsive, defiant, gave us an intolerant stare and disappeared back into the fur coat.

"The surprise is the *postre*," the *Condessa* said. "The dessert. I have a friend," she said, "who took the *Talgo* to Barcelona just for the *postre*."

When the *postre* was served the Peke made a special trip out of the coat to look at it. It was an *helado* shaped like a fountain capped with wild raspberries, brazed almonds and green syrup of figs. The whole thing was still burning from a brandy fire the chef had started in the kitchen. Now it went out and the Peke went home to the coat. The *postre* was too much, but I ate it because the *Condessa* watched. Then there was *galletas* and roquefort, then the perfect black *café-solo* and brandy.

"The *Talgo* will never let anyone know where they get their brandy," the *Condessa* said. "I suspect they make it themselves. There's another rumor they smuggle it in from Italy under a common label. Still, that's what makes life interesting, the mysteries," the *Condessa* said. "Now do you mind if I pay for this?" the *Condessa* said, touching her coat where the dog must be. "After all, you are in Spain. How long have you been in Spain?" the *Condessa* said.

"One day," I said. "Not counting the time we spent in Mallorca."

"No, the Mallorca time should not count," the *Condessa* said. "It is only a tourist place."

We didn't let the *Condessa* pay for the lunch.

"All right, you will not let me be Spanish," the *Condessa* said. "And I will have one of your cigarettes. Good," she said, inhaling deeply and gesturing the waiter to remove the scaffolding in front of us. "Good," she said. "I can stand no talk, not even small talk until I have eaten. Now that I have eaten, what do you think of Franco?"

"We have only been in Spain one day," I said.

"That's true," the *Condessa* said. "What do you think of El Greco?"

"*Estupendo*," Martha said.

"You'll even think more of him after you've been to Toledo," the Condessa said. "What do you do?" the *Condessa* said to me abruptly.

"I write," I said.

"There's nothing to write about in Spain," she said. "We are in an interim period when nothing is happening."

"Between kings," I said.

"That is right," the *Condessa* said. "The usurpers are fighting for the power. As I said, it's an interim period. There's nothing to write about now," the *Condessa* said. "And what do you do?" the *Condessa* said to Martha.

"I paint."

"And there's nothing to paint about either," the *Condessa* said. "So they make dots and marks on canvas or they sprinkle the paint on or they throw the paint on or they walk over a canvas with mud on their shoes or ride a bicycle across it. Sometimes they take a Coca-Cola bottle or reproduce a *Super Hombre* strip, but they do not paint because there's nothing to paint about now. In the old days there was something to paint about. Velasquez painted the aristocrats on fat horses or their narrow children in great wide dresses that covered the canvas, because he believed in the aristocracy. Goya painted the Maja naked—that was the Duke of Alba's wife—because Goya believed in her naked, and he painted the horrors of that time, the Grotesques, not because he believed in the revolution, but because he believed in the person. Goya was saying, *Viva la persona individual*. That's why Goya could paint, because he had something to paint about. Now there's nothing to paint. Now El Greco," the Condessa said, pointing her finger up from the dog, "El Greco was such a *magnifico* because he believed in money. He also believed in prostitutes and he believed in the insane and he had a sense of humor as well as a sense of dignity and a sense of grace, but he was not a religious man, otherwise why would he have used prostitutes for angels and the insane for God? El Greco and Goya did not produce Spain; Spain produced Goya

76

and El Greco and many more, many more. Now we produce a man who makes spots on canvas. Now we produce Miró. Sometimes there is a long line of round objects but mostly it is spots. Do you agree?" the *Condessa* said to Martha.

"They are good spots," Martha said.

"Spots are spots," the *Condessa* said. "Where are you going?" the *Condessa* said.

"I'm going out to get some air," I said.

"I am thinking of giving you a commission," the *Condessa* said. "When you get back we will perhaps talk about it."

The light aluminum cars pitched and rolled like a small boat on the tracks that were not welded. It seemed as though the tracks were not there at all and we were making our way across the vineyards without help. The *Talgo* was pulling into Reus when I got to the bar and sat down. You could see them loading barrels of wine and barrels of olive oil in a long white building near the tracks. They were using horses. None of the roads were paved. There was a huge windmill down the road that was not working. Many young men were sitting around the railway station not working either. I ordered coffee and brandy. Just before the *Talgo* pulled out, a small boy carrying a huge tray strewn with pastry over his head walked close to the train, holding them high as though an offering in some religious procession, but the windows were sealed; the *Talgo* was supposed to be air-conditioned, so he did no business. You'd think that after a few years this boy would have learned, or perhaps having nothing better to do he was showing off his goods.

"This is the poorest place in the world," the bartender said. "I don't know why we stop here. In the last twenty-two years we have not left anyone or taken anyone from Reus."

"You should keep trying," I said.

"That's right," the bartender said. "We shouldn't give up now."

When the train pulled out of Reus I was alone with the bartender in the shiny aluminum room on the shiny aluminum train that joggled like a toy across Spain. Now through the dry yellow fields west of Reus the bartender swept everything that was on the bar onto the floor, then dumped the ash trays too on the floor. It is a custom in Spain that never bothered me but always surprised me. Then he did the same to my table and all the other tables. I suppose at the end of the line they swept the floor. They had a system.

"You don't remember me," the bartender said, making talk. "*No me recuerde.* You were sitting with the *Condessa.* I served the brandy."

"Yes, I remember," I lied.

"The *Condessa* is an old customer of ours," the bartender said. "She makes this trip *frequemente.*"

"Yes," I said. "She is the courier of the king."

"What?" the bartender said. "*Qué?*"

"Nothing," I said.

The bartender had finished throwing everything on the floor and now he went behind the bar where he felt safe.

I finished my coffee and brandy, left the bartender an extra *duro*, got up and made my way through the rubble and down the train that was beginning to hop now, hop hop hop as it raced along, sometimes forgetting the tracks at one hundred miles an hour.

The *Condessa* was preening herself with her long fingers through her blue hair and holding a private and personal conversation with the dog. Martha was holding on without a seat belt and reading *The Life and Works of Sigmund Freud.*

"An amazing man," she said as I sat down.

"Who?" the *Condessa* said, looking up from the dog suddenly. "The king?"

"Of course," I said. Now I said, "Who is the king?"

"Don Juan," the *Condessa* said. "I will show you his picture."

On our first day in Madrid we went to the Prado which was four blocks from our hotel, the *Los Angeles*, and beyond the Plaza del Sol. We were too tired after the Prado, too tired after all that magnificence, too tired to see the *Condessa*, which we had promised we would. But we saw her Ritz which is right next to the Prado, with a huge onion on top and impeccably-kept gardens that still had a few roses in January, but we told ourselves we would see the *Condessa* tomorrow.

The next day we did. The *Condessa* was living way up in the onion of the Ritz, that is, she had a rounded corner living space. You could not call it a room, and you could not even call it a suite; it was more like a private house with even private stairs going up to more bedrooms. On the train, on the *Talgo*, the *Condessa* had been having an adventure and with great daring had been travelling alone. Now she was rescued by her maids. God knows what might have happened to her out there all alone, but now she was ensconced in the phalanx of her maids in the onion of the Ritz, preened and always followed about by one of them. There were three. The *Condessa* had probably seen better days when there were more. Now there were three.

After she told us how delighted she was that we had at last come she said, "I'm sorry that William is not here." About ten minutes later when William arrived I gathered that William was the butler who should have opened the door for us, who had been down checking the fresh antimacassars and tidies that had not been there for our arrival. William wore full dress and white tie, but his elegance was subdued in a gentlemanly reserved intimacy that made guests feel they were not charity cases brought in from the street by the *Condessa*.

"We must have tea," the *Condessa* said. "But there are too many here," she said looking around at the servants. "They are still getting ready for my arrival. We must go below in the ballroom. We can have privacy there."

The ballroom of the Ritz looked like part of the great lobby. It looked much larger than it was because it was mirrored at both ends, which not only gave it the illusion of being larger but of having twice as many people as there were. It also gave the waiters in full dress an opportunity to admire themselves every time they turned around which they did often. I looked over the vast room which grew not only lemon trees, orange trees, banana and date trees, but something that looked as though it were growing coconuts. Light filtered through an enormous roof in stained glass like a church. You expected the waiter was going to say the Mass, but he was more serious than that when he served us the bread of his flesh and the wine of his blood, the tea and cakes. Some of the cakes were topped with cream, raspberry tortes in brandy and something that seemed to be the *specialité* of the Ritz and that the *Condessa* always demanded, ginger nuts with flecks of silver and gold.

"You can get by at the Ritz," the *Condessa* said, "for fifty dollars a day. There are two of you, so for you it would be much less."

"If there were three of us we could make money," I said.

"The Ritz is so close to the Prado Museum," the *Condessa* said, "that you can see the Murillos from your window."

"If anyone wants to," I said.

"Oh, he's really not that bad," the *Condessa* said, and then she said quickly without taking her eyes, her shining clear, cold eyes, off us, her eyes as bright as the Ritz. "I'm thinking of entrusting you with the king's message."

All of the Ritz waiters glanced at each other. They all wore hard shirts under their full dress. Some had clean red stripes on their hard shirts and some had blue stripes on their hard shirts. I suppose it all had something to do with what company or what service they performed in the army of the Ritz. All of them wore tails that touched their ankles. All of them walked with a swinging strut *à la* Charlie Chaplin. They must have learned it at some West Point of waiters. Now that the *Condessa* was about to commission us in service to the king, they all gave each other this quick glance, more a salute, to show that they knew what others did not know. The waiters of the Ritz must be for the Monarchists, the Praetorian Guard, the Last Redoubt, the Final Keep.

"I have been thinking about you," the *Condessa* said. "Ever since I met you on the train. Whether or not I could entrust the king's message to you." She held up a ginger nut and savored it. "I have decided that I can."

"Who is the message for?"

"I am not at liberty to tell you that," the *Condessa* said, putting down the ginger nut with a slight bang. "Still, don't get the idea that this is a Hitchcock film. There is no Orient Express, no naked ladies in upper berths."

80

"If we took the message, when would we get it?"

"I'm not at liberty to tell you that," the *Condessa* said with enough assurance to pick up her ginger nut again. And then she said, to soothe our feelings—she must have planned this but wanted to say it at exactly the right time—"William will be at liberty tomorrow to take you to Toledo to see the El Grecos."

"But we were going to take a Pullmantur, a sightseeing bus to Toledo."

"You can't see the El Grecos from a sightseeing bus."

"But they will let us out."

"William will let you out as well," the *Condessa* said firmly, eating all of her ginger nut. And that was that.

"What time do you want William to call?"

"I'm not at liberty—. What about eight?"

"William will have the Rolls there at eight. Where are you staying?"

"The *Los Angeles*."

"What's that?" the *Condessa* said, startled. "I never heard of it. Very well," the *Condessa* said quietly and firmly, all of her ginger nuts gone. "William at eight o'clock."

Back at the *Los Angeles*, filled full of ginger nuts, we decided we should put off dinner till later. We did not realize then that dinner in Madrid begins at nine and that you can get a dinner at midnight, so when we arrived late at the *Callejon*, eight o'clock, it was too early, so we had Martinis. In Madrid a Martini is exactly that, a glass of Martini and Rossi vermouth with a taste of gin. Then we had a good dinner and next morning got up early to wait for William. Even in a hotel like the *Los Angeles* they employ myriads of sallow, pinch-faced youngsters who open doors for you, run elevators, carry messages and get in the way. The hotel was run by uniformed children, not dwarfs or midgets, but fourteen-year-olds who worked twelve hours a day for eighty-five cents and had to mend and press their own uniforms. No school. The hotel was run by illiterate children. In the lobby the uniformed William towered above the uniformed children as though he were about to rally them for one last charge of the citadel of poverty, neglect and indifference, but he only said, "The Condessa Maria Theresa

Vilchez-Morillo y Diaz Muriana wishes me to tell you that if you care to take her with you to Toledo, the Condessa Maria Theresa Vilchez-Morillo y Diaz Muriana is at liberty."

"The time it took you to say that name," I said, "we could have been to Toledo and back. Of course we will take her," I said. "It's her Rolls, her William."

You can see the onion on top of the Ritz from anywhere in Madrid and it guides you like a mosque from Mecca. When we got to the Ritz the *Condessa* was waiting, surrounded by her Ritz guard of uniformed children. William got out and helped her in and the *Condessa* said, "This is a treat. *Un regalo. Un placer.* I haven't been to Toledo since the *Marquis* was here."

We drove out by the Campo del Moro, crossing the Rio Manzanares near the Ronda to the old Arab quarter until we passed the ancient Toledo Gate, then we had to go back because the *Condessa* remembered we had not seen the Goyas at the Florida. The Florida Chapel was a small, innocent-looking seventeenth century domed building that didn't look as though it held any Goya treasures, but it did, and it contained his body too. There is only one not very large room in the small building and the Goya masterpiece is up in the dome. It is Christ raising the dead, and the spectators are all leaning over a balcony to watch. Most of them did not seem too impressed by the miracle. Two little boys are kicking each other and a woman is primping herself. The whores are going about their business, and on the far side of the balcony someone who is not involved in the miracle is standing up and trying to attract attention to himself. While all this is going on in the dome of the *Monasterio*, Goya is lying quietly beneath a marble slab below, the same position and place he must have occupied while he was estimating the work.

The aged retainer said, "Without the head. Goya's body was brought here about one hundred years ago from Bordeaux, France, where he died, but without the head. Goya must have lost his head over some French girl." That was the aged retainer's joke for the day. And then he said, "You can see the Goyas better from the *espejos.*"

The *espejos* were four mirrors placed at standing height, angled up at the paintings so you could examine the Goya mural without craning your neck. We had a good look and thought it was worth the trip back, worth the trip to Spain. Then we tipped the aged retainer who had no more jokes and left with the *Condessa* who turned on the TV as soon as we got in the car. The TV set was built into the rear of the front seat and concealed in a small ivory panel. There was an antenna that appeared in the roof of the Rolls when she pressed a silver button, then she asked William to back the car up and turn the car slightly to the left so she could get a better picture. William had to back up over a parking ramp until one wheel was up in the air and he asked her how that was.

"Perfect," she said. "Look," she said to us. "Churchill's funeral. Take a good look," she said. "We'll lose the picture as soon as we get on the Toledo road."

And we did too.

"I love gadgets," the *Condessa* said. "That's what I like about Americans."

The road to Toledo goes over a brown undulating limestone plain with a very thin layer of topsoil which is entirely blown away in spots, revealing a whiteness that in a distance looks like large lakes.

"At one time," the *Condessa* said, "Toledo was where the kings lived, so it has a warm spot for me. It wasn't until the seventeenth century that they came to Madrid. Because of the climate," the *Condessa* said. "That reminds me," the *Condessa* said, "you are going to deliver the message for me, aren't you?"

"That's right."

"I've had a chance to think it over," the *Condessa* said, "and I'm at liberty to tell you that you will do."

"Thank you."

"Good," she said, touching us both with her long fingers. "Where are we?" she asked William.

"Torrejon de la Calzada."

"Then we have a long way to go," the *Condessa* said.

In Toledo the *Condessa* insisted we get a guide. It was lunch time and we had not eaten yet, but as soon as we had crossed the

Rio Tajo that separates Toledo from the plains she insisted we get a guide because, although she knew Toledo before the war, much of it was destroyed during the war and probably most of the good restaurants were affected, she said. We got a guide on the Plaza Zocadover who took us to a small restaurant near the Alcazar which was good. Toledo is a high promontory of rock surrounded by a loop of the Rio Tajo, so from way up there in the sidewalk café outside the Alcazar we could see a vast distance across the dry plains.

"I think I could get a good picture up here," the *Condessa* said and went over to the Rolls to try. William backed and filled the car around the square, trying to get in the right position, but the *Condessa* came back defeated.

"I can't get any picture at all up here," she said. "I wonder how Churchill is doing."

William ate a lunch which he had brought along in the car, which gave him a privacy and a kind of nobility as he ate in the Rolls, a kind of snobbery. After lunch we went inside the Alcazar, our guide showing the way. Our guide was a small, nimble hunchback. He said his name was Pedro Macho Cabrío, Pete the Goat, which I thought described him pretty well. The Alcazar was still being rebuilt and our guide explained to us that during the war the Fascist troops had held out here for two months until they were relieved by Franco's column. They would never surrender. Then he wanted to show us another room where—. But the *Condessa* said she was bored. "Have you had enough?" the *Condessa* said.

"Yes, we surrender," we said.

Pedro took us back under the scaffolding of the *obreros* who were rebuilding the Alcazar to the Rolls where William had finished his lunch and was back in the rear trying to get something on TV.

"Any luck?" the *Condessa* said.

"No luck," William said, getting back in the front seat.

"Churchill's probably all the way to Westminster Abbey by now," the *Condessa* said.

William drove us down the hill to the church where the greatest El Greco is, the Burial of the Count of Orgaz. The *Condessa* found several of her relatives in the picture and, still pointing, told us who was related to whom and why.

"They wanted to put this picture in a travelling show to America," the *Condessa* said, "but the local *padre* paid El Greco for it, so it's a permanent possession of the priest of this parish and the present *padre* would not let it go. It could never find its way back, the priest said."

Now we went to El Greco's home. El Greco lived well. A relative of the *Condessa* had given the El Greco house to the state. The house was built around a huge patio. El Greco worked on the top floor and entertained the *Condessa's* ancestors below.

"But we should get back to Madrid now," the *Condessa* said. "William doesn't like to drive in the dark."

Because William did not like to drive in the dark, I thought he drove back to Madrid too fast. The *Condessa* got Churchill again, and before she dropped us off at the *Los Angeles*, Churchill was buried. We had agreed to meet tomorrow at the station at one-thirty to catch the train going south.

"On the train," the *Condessa* said, "I can tell you more. Here in Madrid I'm not at liberty to do so."

The first-class compartments of the train were out of Oscar Wilde, early Aubrey Beardsley, with buttercup frosted glass light fixtures and red carpets over the walls. All the fixtures were in gold. You pressed a silver button for the writing desk, and there was a bronze statue of a woman you pulled for the maid and a silver statue of a man you pulled for a man. This way you didn't have to speak Spanish. All the signs were in French: *Le Chaud, Le Froid* for the heater and *Bonjour Messieurs et Mesdames* for welcome sir or madam. Nothing worked. When you pressed the button to let down the table the lights went off, and when you pulled for the maid, water came out from underneath the seats. The *Condessa* had spread all of her things out on the seats instead of putting her luggage up so there was no place for us to sit.

"It's cold in here," Martha said.

"Nothing has worked since the Civil War," the *Condessa* said.

"But that was twenty-five years ago," I said.

"It seems like yesterday," the Condessa said. "*Sientese*," she said. "Sit down," she said, making a hole for us by pushing her things. "Now," she said, leaning back and looking out the window you could not look out of since the war, "What do you think of Spain?" When we hesitated she said, "Feel at liberty to say anything. You know, something happened to me yesterday at Toledo," the Condessa said. "I believe I've always realized the importance of our cause, but yesterday at Toledo those pictures of my relatives reminded me how much we are needed, how much Spain needs us. El Greco was a friend," the Condessa said, "and has kept our cause alive. I'm not at liberty to tell you everything," the Condessa said, "but I can tell you what is already known and add one small piece of information. The king, Don Juan, lives at Estoril in Portugal. His son, the crown prince, Don Carlos, is somewhere in Spain. What I am at liberty to add now," the Condessa said, "is that you very definitely can take the message to Seville."

"What's that?" I said. There was a loud, steady clacking bump.

"Only a flat wheel," the Condessa said.

"It feels to me as though it's bobbling," I said. "About to come off."

"The State runs these trains," the Condessa said. "And as bad as the State is now, nevertheless I suspect that they know how to put on a train wheel so it won't come off."

The wheel came off just this side of Cordova and we had to wait there, a wounded row of ancient cars in the middle of a flat and endless vineyard going on all the way to the flat horizon as far as you could see. A man had left the scene of the wounded train with a string of burros to find a wheel. He got the string of burros from two men he found working the vineyards near the tracks. "The next station is not far," he said, and it would not take him long to find the wheel, but the station was at least as far as the distant horizon, and when the string of burros finally disappeared we settled down for a long wait. The Condessa went to sleep. Cordova was not far off, Cordova where we would separate from the Condessa, so the last opportunity we had to find out all about the monarchy in Spain from the mover and shaker, from the horse's mouth, was slipping away as the *Condessa* slept and the burros plodded to find a wheel.

"The past," the *Condessa* said, wakening, struggling through her sleep to find some meaning in words. "The past?" she said vaguely. "The past. But I'm not at liberty—."

"Not at liberty for what?" I said, touching her and speaking directly and firmly to her. "What is it you are not at liberty—?"

"The ghosts," the *Condessa* said, stroking at the cobwebs of sleep, at the dark curtain. "At Toledo didn't you see them? At the burial of the *Conde de Orgaz*? You were there. Everyone was there. El Greco saw them."

"But what is it you are not at liberty—?"

"One can't take liberties. One can't, you know," she said carefully through the curtain.

"With ghosts?"

Behind the dark red cobweb of sleep, the curtains of the ancient train compartment, the *Condessa* slowly nodded her blue head firmly up and down, but definitely and with dignity.

"Here come the burros. They found a wheel," Martha said.

It took them about three hours to get the wheel on with the small, wise, tough burros who brought the wheel watching it go on. We left them there in the middle of that vast endless vineyard, puffed away behind our steam engine, leaving the vineyard richer by one thousand *pesetas* and the gray burros sagging a little but looking even wiser than before. When we got to Cordova and before the *Condessa* left us for another train that would take her to Malaga, she gave us the message we must take to Seville. It was contained in a medium-sized parchment-like material, sealed in red wax with a crest that was used every day in Toledo a long time ago. Then her maid, who had taken another compartment, came and got her. The *Condessa* had said nothing since the burros had left us for the wheel and she struggled briefly in her sleep to tell us something, probably some information, something improbable and tenuous, a great dark ship against a somber sinking sun, then the Burial of the Count of Orgaz with the angels and all the attendants coming down to get him and all ethereal and luminous. The *Condessa* was borne away now by her maid down the long dusty train

Johnny said that the jaundiced, sickly-faced Gibraltar newspaper man was dying to play. Johnny called him the Yellow Journalist.

We had all come over from Spain, Johnny-Behind-the-Deuce, my wife Martha, and I. We had trouble at the border. The British couldn't let us in and the Spanish wouldn't let us out, so we stood there walking that line. We had rented a car in Seville, reserved a room at the Victoria Hotel in Gibraltar, and now the Spanish Guardia Civil in cocked hat wouldn't let our car through.

"Why not?" my wife Martha said.

"Politics," the Guardia Civil said. "We let twenty cars a day through, that's all."

Johnny-Behind-the-Deuce leaned on the guard line. He was a young gentleman who had never been in a war and I was afraid he was going to make a dash for it. He was a young man with a thin beard who had read a lot and not learned much. He had recommended the rental car in Seville, said he could drive it expertly and couldn't, said he knew how to get to Gibraltar and didn't, said he played cards for a living and did. He was a young man whose father owned a small mountain of buried coal in Ohio and hoped that one day his son would help him move it. But Johnny-Behind-the-Deuce did not find moving a mountain interesting. But take a good game of cards—take a fast-moving nether finger, a quicksilver finger faster than light—. Johnny also had explained to us that there would be this trouble at the border.

Johnny made a quick jump over the Line, over the black and white striped guard rail that goes up and down like scissors. Johnny flew down the concrete ramp that goes around the tank traps in front of the British air strip, and then, before anyone could move, he was in the arms of the British. The Spanish Guardia Civil in charge did not have enough time to exhale the lungful of smoke from his twisted cigarette before Johnny was safely on the Rock. Martha and I got over there slowly and legally.

"Yes, I believe the Yellow Journalist is dying to play," Johnny said.

The lobby of the Victoria Hotel in Gibraltar looks like a B movie set for a picture about the Colonies. While we sat there some Russians came in. They had been wandering around town all morning. Their freighter, the Maxim Gorki, had tied up to refuel at 3:30 that morning. The Russian crew came ashore in relays and the Captain showed each bunch around. He waddled in the middle of them, a short, square man showing them the sights.

Johnny-Behind-the-Deuce lit a long, slim and black cigar. "The Darlings are arriving this afternoon," Johnny said.

"Who are the Darlings?" Martha said.

"A singing group, the same as the Beatles," Johnny-Behind-the-Deuce said.

"Who are the Beatles?"

"Cute children with a drum," Johnny-Behind-the-Deuce said, "but I think the Darlings might want to play some poker. They're on their way to Australia where they will be attacked by the teenage girls. They will stay in Gibraltar two days. Isn't that right?" Johnny-Behind-the-Deuce said, looking up and over at the Yellow Journalist. The Yellow Journalist was standing by the reception desk. He had been introduced to us as the editor of a local paper.

"The Darlings," Johnny-Behind-the-Deuce said quietly to us over his long slim cigar, "should be bored on the Rock, want to play a little poker." Then he said dreamily, "It seems to me that if I could get the Darlings, the Yellow Journalist, the Russian Captain and maybe one or two members of his crew we could have a good game. That's the problem on the Rock, there is absolutely nothing to do. Don't you suppose they'd even be willing to lose some money? What do you suppose—," Johnny-Behind-the-Deuce said, "what do you suppose the Russians use for money?"

That afternoon we took the tour of the Rock in a Volkswagen omnibus. The Volkswagen got its passengers from the three hotels in town, the Queen's, the Rock, the Victoria. The Yellow Journalist saw us off, watching from his eyrie at the hotel desk. The tour consisted of the hill to the Gibraltar apes, the hill to the fortress and the hill to the water collection point. The Russian Captain and his bewhiskered crew were making the tour on foot. The Russian Captain and his crew were better on the hills than the Volkswagen. Going down the hills we could almost catch the Captain and his crew, but going up the hills the Volkswagen had to gear down too much to keep up.

We were stopping now for the apes. The apes got to Gibraltar from Africa when the land mass was continuous, or when they swam across the straits, or when they came over under the straits through a secret ape tunnel which no one has ever been able to find. These are the three theories. Now one of the apes with a wide bottom was sitting over the entrance to the maybe secret tunnel, hiding it, shielding the route to Africa. When we got out of the bus the ape ambled off the secret tunnel entrance, came over to Martha, pulled off her pearls and tried them on. It must have been a lady ape. Martha swung at the lady ape with her Double Crostic board.

"Don't accost the apes, Madam," the British guard said.

"I didn't accost her," Martha said. "I swung at her. She's got my pearls."

"I have not," the lady ape said. She said it by folding her arms on her breast and looking at Martha askance.

"And where did you get those pearls?" the British guard said to the lady Gibraltar ape. The lady ape tolerated him and the British guard removed the pearls from the lady ape and put them back on Martha.

Johnny-Behind-the-Deuce was looking over the parapet of the gun pit along with the rest of the apes. Down at the air strip where the Darlings would arrive. There were some military vehicles on the apron of the air strip waiting. The Gibraltar air strip was placed across the short causeway to Spain. Spain complained when the British built the air strip because it is man-made and encroaches on their water. "*Our* water," the British said. But now the cold war had stopped, so both sides could watch the Beatles—the Darlings—arrive. The primates on both sides of the border were tense and expectant. All the apes standing near us kept their cool, except the ape who had stolen Martha's pearls. She held her left foot in her mouth with her right hand and jumped up and down on her right foot, which is lady ape language for Go Go Go, as she watched down at the airport for the Darlings' plane.

The Yellow Journalist's red Jaguar pulled up to the apron of the air strip now. He got out and waited with his notebook. The Yellow Journalist was impatient and paced up and down. Excepting the lady ape, all the primates around us kept their calm and dignity in the face of the arriving Darlings. Johnny-Behind-the-Deuce offered one of the men apes a cigar. The man ape took it and ate it, but not before offering half of it to a comrade, so Charles Darwin was wrong. "Charles Darwin was wrong about a lot of things," the ape man said, seemed to say, as he sat on the parapet next to Wellington's cannon and looked down at the people waiting for the Darlings.

"You wouldn't be interested in a game of poker?" Johnny-Behind-the-Deuce said. The Charles Darwin ape spat some of the cigar on the cannon, clapped his hands, signalled the gun to fire and then held his ears. It was an old routine, but it still got a laugh out of the apes, including us.

The Darlings' plane was spotted now, a high distant speck over the sands of North Africa, and a majestic scream went up from both sides of the border. As the plane circled Gibraltar another mighty scream arose, then it circled Spain and seven dueñas committed suicide, and as the plane made its landing approach the female Gibraltar apes ran amok, killing all the tourists. As the plane came to a halt the Yellow Journalist went out to the plane as the Darlings came off. The Darlings had never been to the Rock before and the sight of it bored them.

"Perfect set-up for a game," Johnny-Behind-the-Deuce said.

The male Darlings wore their hair like women or like fifteenth century knights. "There were no knights in the fifteenth century," Martha said. "Oh, I think it's interesting that the British have held Gibraltar longer than the Spanish have held it. The Spanish took it from the Arabs in 711 and lost it to the British in 1603. Of course the British have held it till now, so you see the Spanish—."

"That should settle their hash," the Charles Darwin ape said, appeared to say, as he pushed us aside and stared down at the Darlings.

93

"Has everyone had quite enough?" the guide said, moving us towards our Volkswagen. One of the apes made a sawing motion at his throat to show that he had had enough up to here as we got on the bus and drove off, leaving the apes staring down at the Darlings. What hath man wrought? I noticed that as the Volkswagen groaned off, the lady ape that had greeted us was seated again at the secret tunnel entrance to Africa where her ancestors had made it over before the Arabs even, before the British.

"Have you got your pearls?"

"Yes," Martha said, fingering them.

After the apes and the water catchments there is nothing else to do or see on Gibraltar, so Johnny's poker game began at ten that evening. There was the Yellow Journalist, the Russian Captain and his Mate who both spoke English, and the four Darlings. Johnny-Behind-the-Deuce dealt. It was stud. The Russian Captain checked his queen, and Johnny-Behind-the-Deuce bet six shillings.

"But you only have a two showing," the Captain said to Johnny-Behind-the-Deuce. The Darlings dropped out and so did the Yellow Journalist. I turned my cards over. The Captain put in six shillings, then raised Johnny a mere sixpence. Johnny-Behind-the-Deuce tossed his deuce and said to the Captain, "You win."

Now it was the first Darling's deal. He wore his hair in a boyish bob, smoked a Jamaica cigar. He had a long, thin, young face. He looked like Prince Valiant. He shuffled the cards like a pro and hummed, "Around the world in eighty days." Now he paused as though trying to recall the lyrics.

"Play cards," the Yellow Journalist said.

"Around the world I'll search for you," Prince Valiant mused. "When love is gone I'll travel on—"

"To keep a *rendezvous*," the final Darling said.

"I quit," the Yellow Journalist said, standing up.

"Cool it," a Darling said in a tough voice and he dealt the Yellow Journalist a card. The Yellow Journalist sat down. When two cards were dealt the Russian sea captain said to Johnny, looking at his show card, "You didn't get a two this time. He didn't get a two this time," the Captain repeated to his First Mate.

"He wasn't dealing this time," his First Mate said.

I don't remember who won this pot. It was small, only about two pounds ten. I think it was one of the Darlings. Anyway there was an underlying tension beginning to build now, a kind of awkward stiffness that begins to build to a point where it almost becomes breathless, when you know the players are maneuvering to set up the game for a kill.

"I bet eight shillings," the Captain said. He tossed them out. Everybody saw him.

After the next round the Yellow Journalist said to the Captain, "You're still high."

"I'll check," the Captain said.

"I bet ten pounds," the Yellow Journalist said. No one "saw" him and the Yellow Journalist drew in the pot without showing his hand. When it came Johnny's turn to deal he dealt himself another two for a face card.

"There is a Russian proverb," the Captain said, waiting for his cards. "There is a Russian proverb that says it is better to be thrown into Hell than to wait too long at the gates of Paradise."

The Maxim Gorki Mate said, half under his breath, "In America you have a saying, Many hands make light work. In Russia we have a saying, Many hands make a crooked game. If he can deal himself a two every time—."

"Don't push it too far," I said. "The deuce may be a coincidence."

"Oh yes!" the Mate said.

"There is a Russian saying—" the Captain said.

"Please," the First Mate said to his Captain, touching his hand. "We'll play these cards first."

The Mate won this hand. The pot was big. Johnny and I dropped out early. The Darlings contributed a lot to it, although the Journalist who stuck it out lost the most—twenty-three pounds.

"Now," the Russian mate said, stacking his notes in one pile, the shillings and pence in another. "What were you saying, Captain?"

"The saying is no longer appropriate," the Captain said.

There were several small pots and then Johnny dealt a hand again.

"There's that two again," the Mate said.

The Journalist bet ten pounds on his ace. Johnny saw him with his deuce. The Journalist raised fifteen pounds. Johnny saw him. The Journalist shuffled his cards, then stared at the ceiling. I got up to get a drink and noticed that the Journalist was holding an ace in his hand plus his ace showing on the table. Johnny put in fifteen more pounds and dealt the Journalist another card as I was standing there, another ace.

"Well, well," the Journalist said quietly. "Well, well, well. In for a penny, in for a pound," and he pushed in twenty-five pounds.

"Okay," Johnny-Behind-the-Deuce said. "I'll stay and raise one."

"And twenty-five more," the Journalist said, dealing the five pound notes out separately like a bank teller. Johnny placed some notes on the pile. The Journalist checked them by riffing them, then he said, "Deal." Johnny gave the Journalist another down card. The Journalist pulled the card up slowly and when he saw it his hand trembled.

"The ace bets," the Mate said.

"Fifty pounds," the Journalist said.

"And one hundred pounds more," Johnny said, counting in the money slowly, dramatically.

"Here's your hundred," the Journalist said, "and it will cost you one hundred and fifty more." He put that in.

Johnny picked up the card he had given himself, looked at it for the first time, stared at it, then he looked at the money. Some of the money was stacked in neat sheaves, the recent money was tossed like green leaves

"There must be twenty-three hundred dollars there," Johnny said. "And you want four hundred more. Tell me, what are you going to do with all that money?"

The Journalist took out his handkerchief, a big gray one, and wiped his forehead, but the sweat came out again immediately in big pinpoints. "Play cards," the Journalist said.

"What are you going to do with all that money?" Johnny said.

I never heard such a big silence before. It was like something before the beginning of the world, or the end. Everything that Johnny-Behind-the-Deuce said was as though spoken in an echo chamber.

"What are you going to do with that money?"

"Get out of this hole. Get off the Rock."

"It's your home?"

"Yes."

"And you knock it?"

The Journalist looked up at the tin ceiling, watched the big fan turn slowly. "I have one card coming."

Johnny dealt him the card. Johnny dealt himself a card.

"Ace bets," I said to the Journalist.

"A thousand pounds."

"I'll see you," Johnny said. There was a big pause, then – "And raise you what I've got."

"What's that?"

"Six shillings tuppence." Johnny put it all out. The Journalist put in his thousand pounds. "I've only got four shillings left."

Johnny took back two shillings tuppence. "Now you can leave home," Johnny said.

"Four aces," the Journalist said.

"I've got a two and a five and a three and a four and here's a six, all black and all spades," Johnny said.

The Journalist took out his gray handkerchief again. It looked awfully big now. It could have hidden a knife or a gun, but as he raised it to his forehead it dangled loose, there was nothing in it, and the handkerchief never got to his forehead. It dangled in the air long seconds, then fell to the table, then his head came down, then everything began to slide; he was slumping off his chair. He just slid onto the floor like a dummy, something that no longer worked.

We got him to the red couch, all of us. Prince Valiant and the Captain were at his head and the Darlings continued to wipe the Journalist's forehead, what the Journalist had been trying to do when his body quit, but the sweat wasn't appearing any more, and his skin wasn't yellowish any more; it was off-gray. You had to keep putting things back on the couch; his arms and legs wanted to fall, dangle lifeless like a marionette.

The Captain and his crew got off the next day without Russian proverbs, but with a load of British fuel. The Captain waved from the bridge as the ship, the Maxim Gorki, disappeared in the mist. We left the next day too, on a boat for Mallorca. Johnny-Behind-the-Deuce didn't try to start a game on the trip to Mallorca. He had provocations from an Arab crew on the fo'c's'le, but he declined.

"I could try the Seychelles," Johnny said. "Then I understand there's another Crown Colony in Hong Kong where a −." Johnny hesitated, his voice weak and cracked. "Where a loser, where a loser doesn't−"

"The point is, he was dying to play," I said. "It wasn't your fault, Johnny."

In the middle of the Straits there is a point at which you can see the North African Spanish port of Ceuta and back to Gibraltar.

"But I guess I'll go home first," Johnny said. "Around the world I'll search for you," Johnny-Behind-the-Deuce said. "When love is gone I'll travel on. But I guess I'll go home first," the man behind the deuce said.

"To move that mountain for the coal?"

"Why not?" Johnny looked at us and through us to the Rock. "Why not?"

DEAD MAN'S GUIDE
TO MALLORCA

39°35″

2°39″

"During the Spanish Civil War," Dr. Villanueva told us on the *terrasse* of the Hotel Londres, "the Italians, Mussolini, took this Loyalist island, Mallorca, for Mr. Franco. We are not far from the Spanish mainland here, about forty miles. It was an excellent base from which to bomb the Loyalist government at Barcelona, and this the Italians did every morning with big Savoia Marchetti bombers. The Marchettis had three engines. They were very powerful and always quite low when they flew over my house. I could see the pilots' faces. But the bombing was a small part of it. It was the terror that was the thing. While the Italian military was in charge it was not so bad, but then Mussolini sent his own man from the Fascist Party. He was a Black Shirt Party man called Rossi. That began the terror. Every night there were at least fifteen killings. The Italians would cover the countryside in trucks, kicking in doors, take the whole family sometimes, kill them near the cemetery so they could be buried easily in the morning. Every afternoon Rossi would drive crazy through Palma in an open Lancia. He always had a general on one side of him and a priest on the other. I guess the priest was to legitimize his moral insanity. Rossi was always putting generals in prison, so each time he drove through Palma he had a different Italian general. The priest's name was Cadello. I knew him; he was a Franciscan. The order wears brown robes and these were always trailing out from the Lancia. Rossi had Father Cadello shot before Rossi returned to Italy. From this *terrasse* you could watch the prison ships at night; Rossi had them all lit up. The prisoners were not fed and most died. The bodies would float in to the beach here in the morning but the families did not dare claim them.

"Yes," Dr. Villanueva said. "Yes. While we were bombing the government of Barcelona—. Because I am alive I say we bombed them, but what could we do?" Dr. Villanueva opened wide his hand and looked out again in the direction of Barcelona. "I think this is typical," he said. "The government anarchists in Barcelona held the telephone exchange and when the President of the Republic called the Prime Minister of the Republic and they had been talking for five minutes the anarchist's voice from the telephone exchange interrupted them. 'Listen,' he said. 'You are boring us.

We are no longer interested in your talk. Stop boring us and hang up!' The Prime Minister and the President hung up." Dr. Villanueva ran his delicate fingers along his heavy chair. "That," he said, "is what we were bombing. But we should not talk about this now," he said.

"You brought it up," I said.

"Yes," Dr. Villanueva said. "But we are supposed to be gay, carefree Spaniards. You notice we always sing while we work. It is not that we are forbidden to talk about this. We are discouraged but not forbidden to talk about this. I suppose it is a medical thing, a psychosis, a block, that has affected a whole people. We cannot yet talk about it because we cannot free ourselves from our past. It is only when we can talk about it that we will be a people again."

"But certainly among yourselves –."

"I believe very little," Dr. Villanueva said. "They have not found a way yet that it can be discussed without opening up ugly wounds in the mind. That hurts very much," Dr. Villanueva said. "It is not a Spanish problem, it is a human problem." Dr. Villanueva looked at his watch. "But I have talked enough about it. That is all the therapy I will have for today."

We had met Dr. Villanueva the second day we were on Mallorca. Martha was still suffering from something she caught at Casablanca and the Hotel Londres had given us Dr. Villanueva's address. He said that almost everyone caught this at Casablanca and he gave her a pill. He wanted to talk in English. He said his therapy had not reached the point where he could talk about Spain in Spanish. When he learned I was a writer he was curious about that. He said, "Our writers write about nothing." And he said, "What is there to write about?" He said, "When people have no past how can they have a future? You can have a kind of present," he said. "You can sing, talk about the weather and the bull fights. That's about it," Dr. Villanueva said. "Did you know that I too was a Fascist?" This had come out quickly and I figured he had been planning it for quite a while. He had wanted to get it off his chest. There was no proper way to say it so he had blurted it out.

"I was very young then," Dr. Villanueva said. "Now I do not know what I am. The easiest thing to say in Spain is that you are a Monarchist. You will hear that frequently on the mainland, but what does that mean in this day and age? It means nothing. It means I do not think. It means I refuse to think." He paused. "Yes, death is the goal of life," he said. And then he said, "I do not tell you about all this because you are a writer but because you are a foreign person. What will you write about? Nothing happens on Mallorca. What will you write about? I can tell you where to go and what and who to see, but what will you write about?"

"I don't know," I said.

"Later you will know," he said. "And your Martha? She is your collaborator?"

"More than that," I said. "Much more. She does the spelling and the typing."

"*Pobre Marta*," Dr. Villanueva said. "*Pobre Marta brava.*" He paused again, staring blankly at the end of his cigarette. "Something did happen once upon a time. But we must not think about it. I refuse to think."

Poor brave Martha and I left Dr. Villanueva who was still refusing to think and rented a car to take a drive around the island. The car rents for two hundred and thirty *pesetas*, about five dollars, plus gas, but with unlimited mileage. They are Seat 600s with a water-cooled engine in the rear, about 35 horse-power, but as an Englishman told me, "They are nippy," and they are excellent for the narrow roads of Mallorca with hairpin turns in the mountains.

Speaking of the English, they have taken over Mallorca. Having quit all the colonies they have founded a redoubt here in a part of Palma called Torrena beneath a Fourteenth Century castle. Their fortress is the Gran Hotel Bretaña. The first impression you get of the British is that they are insensitive and arrogant. Yesterday there was an English lady on the *terrasse* of the Gran Bretaña that overlooks the harbor in the direction of Ibiza. She was complaining about the weak tea to a Mallorcan official who was trying to explain to her that now, after six months, her visa would have to be renewed, and between complaints about the weak tea she kept saying in a strict voice, "No, no. I haven't the time. This will cause Spain trouble. Very much trouble. You will be punished for this. Oh, yes, the Spanish will be punished," she said, waving her long arm vaguely in the direction of Gibraltar.

I said the British arrogance and insensitiveness is the first impression, but the big thing is they have a sense of humor about themselves. Not a humor directed cruelly at other people, but a humor about themselves. There will always be a duchess on the *terrasse* waving the Spanish government vaguely toward Gibraltar, but the duchess will give you a wink when she does it. "Oh, I may be a bit of a fool, but I am enjoying it very much, thank you. Americans, I believe? Strange people. Strange people, the Americans."

We swept past the duchess now, bounded past the duchess in our Seat and made it out of town towards Inca on the Via Puerta road. We were going to Puerta de Pollensa near the Cabo Formentor to a pension on the beach run by a Señora Tarrogona that the doctor had recommended. The island is about forty-five miles long and thirty miles wide. We were going down the length, down the spine of the mountains along the west coast. We went through a town called Valdemosa and Martha asked me why we didn't stop. "The glass factory," she said.

So we went back and saw the glass factory. It was a dungeon in a medieval setting, emitting a tall pillar of smoke and filming up, shooting out myriad stars of light from a molten crucible surrounded by small boy workers, children in the brilliant light, each gathering a ball of molten glass at the end of a sword stick and bearing it away like a giant lollipop to the maestro who gathered it and blew it, at the end of a pipe he played, into a shimmering globe of light. Now he kneaded it on the anvil into a vinegar carafe with quick Cellini movements while the child went back to the crucible and returned bearing more glittering taffy. This was dropped by the Maestro, a thin stem of it, on each side of the carafe making the point of contact hot enough, weak enough, so that when he blew into his carafe again a hole appeared into the stems. More blowing and they became tear-shaped and hollow, then he waited long seconds until they were brittle and clipped them off with a knock on the anvil, and he had an oil or vinegar carafe fit for the Borgias, selling for two hundred *pesetas*—three dollars and eighty cents; more than the children got each day, more than the maestro. In the half hour we were there the children and the maestro made six of them.

"But there are difficulties and expenses," the *dueño*, the owner, told us. He was standing amidst the shattered Coca-Cola bottles his art was made of. "Then too," he said, "something of quality does not always sell."

We bought one of them to show him that they sometimes did, and made our way back to the Seat through the crowd of children bearing more baked red apples of glass on sticks.

When we got back to the Seat Martha said, "While we're in Valdemosa we should go and see the monastery where George Sand and Chopin lived."

"Do you think you can make it?" I said. "Chopin lived there and said it was cold and dank and the roof leaked. Do you feel up to it?"

"I don't feel up to it but I can make it," Poor Brave Martha said.

I had always imagined a forlorn pile of rocks on a lonely mountainside. The monastery stood alongside the church and was right in town. There was a narrow road that swept around the mountain and up to an escarpment where the monastery was. It was the same trail that George Sand had got Chopin's piano up when he complained about the lack of this instrument. She tried to fix the roof when he complained about that, and did her best to get some heat when he complained about the cold. When he complained about her cigar butts in the bedroom she just threw rocks at him. Anyway, that's the way the story goes that brings the visitors here. There are so many romantic legends, so many spiritual myths that Valdemosa has decided to go with a tough one, so they had it that George Sand conned Chopin into coming down here under the pretext it would cure his T.B., that it was a beautiful warm monastery in the sun where the peasants danced all night and the burros were so sweet they melted at a touch. She hadn't mentioned a leaky roof or her cigar butts and when Chopin wanted out there was no boat so he spent his lonely hours in a wistful vigil on the turret tower of the monastery watching for a sail that would take him back to Paris, but there was only the distant pillar of smoke moving up the mountainside of Valdemosa as George Sand made her way back to the bedroom with a Corona-Corona.

The interior of the monastery was a magnificent sight, vast vaulting corridors, noble and endless, running off fountain and Arabic-tiled patios, a riot of mosaic. The fountains were working now. They hadn't been when Chopin was there. He had complained about that too. Off the Gothic fluted corridors were the rooms where the lovers had dwelt, opening out on magic casements and the distant sea. Each room had a guide dressed in silk medieval costume to tell you what happened there. There hadn't been any medieval costumes in 1840 when the lovers were here but it looked good. The first room we went into was a study that kept all the books that George Sand had written. The guide was looking out the magic casements, a young girl in a red turban picking her nose and blowing a bubble with bubble gum that was already as big as the window. We left before it burst. We went into the room where all the trouble had begun, the reason for the trip, the failure, the success, the gossip, the *Champs de Mars*, the bedroom. The room was pristine, tidy, impeccable, with all the cigar ash tidied up.

"It shows you what a hundred years can do," Poor Brave Martha said.

A child guide was asleep on the bed, her moccasin shoes out of J.C. Penney soiling the counterpane. She will hear from Chopin about this, not George. Evidently George Sand would take anything.

We were out in the vaulted hall again. George Sand had exquisite taste in monasteries and perhaps in lovers too. We would never know. It would be the big secret the ruins never revealed. On the way out the child who had blown herself up with the bubble gum was waiting for a tip. She had a Walt Disney Donald Duck watch on her wrist as she extended her olive hand. I gave her a *duro*, five *pesetas*, and we were off in a cloud of children who had come running, but too late, when they discovered there were Americans. My last view, my last memory was the child guide blowing another huge bubble into which the ghost of Chopin stepped, then exploded in a cloud of smoke.

Poor Brave Martha had stood up well. When she closed the door of the Seat it came off, but on our trip to Deya she held the whole car together with her will power. Deya is the town of poets. Robert Graves lives here and a cult, a covey, of poets has settled in the foothills. Deya clings to the sides of precipitous rock-strewn, uninteresting hills and the only inspiration you could get is the thought of getting out. For local color there is a gas station from which it is impossible to get gas if another car is coming down the cliff. We found this out and decided to try to make it to Pollensa before we filled up. My memory of Deya is not good but it must be a fine place for poets.

Before we got to Pollensa we ran out of gas and Poor Brave Martha got out and pushed. "If you can just make it up that rise," I said, "just one more little rise and we can sail into Pollensa. It's all down hill." But it was an optical illusion. When finally we did get going into Pollensa and Martha was inside with the Seat door on her lap she said she was beat. "Now I know how Chopin felt," she said.

There was a gas station before we got to Pollensa. It was on a slight rise but we swept up to it and got to the pump using gravity. I went inside and had an anise. Poor Brave Martha had a Pepsi-Cola. I asked her how it was. After the first sip she said it was better than anywhere else. "It may be that it was just a good year," I said. "It probably doesn't ship well."

The owner came in now with a friend who had a dog. The man with the dog said the dog was very intelligent and could understand six languages. The man ordered a cup of coffee and gave one of his two sugars to the dog. I thought the dog took the sugar very intelligently. I told the man with the dog that out here in the hills was probably not a good place for a precocious dog. In the city there would be more opportunities, I said. The owner of the station felt out of it and he brought out a bird in a cage that he said was very intelligent. It was a mountain thrush and he said it was more intelligent than any dog. I thought the dog owner took this well. Martha took some more of the Pepsi-Cola and couldn't make up her mind. "The mountain thrush," I said. "How many languages does he speak?"

"None," the bird owner said. "Why should he bother?"

"That's very intelligent of him," I said. "He's probably an Existentialist bird."

"What else?" the bird owner said.

"Or something worse," the dog owner said, fighting back for the first time. Poor Brave Martha took another sip of Pepsi-Cola and said she was going to be sick. The dog owner insisted we go up on the roof and see the ocean five miles away. "In the other direction you can see the poets," he said. "And the house of George Sand and the man who played the piano. But that was a long time ago," he said with a sigh, as though there were no need for us to go on the roof.

"But the poets are still there I think," the bird owner said.

Poor Brave Martha was picking up the door of the Seat when we got out, and arranging it on the side of the car. "I'm warning you," she said as we swept down the hills to Pollensa. "Don't run out of gas again. That's the last time I'll push."

"Which was the best," I said, "the dog or the bird?"

"The Pepsi-Cola," she said. "It ships better than you think."

The Puerta de Pollensa is a miniature harbor that lies just below the break in the mountains. Cola San Vicente and the Pension Ultimo of Señora Tarragona, according to Dr. Villanueva, was somewhere close. "Muy cerca." We found it at the bottom of a granite canyon just off the harbor. It had a private white beach that shimmered from way up. Poor Brave Martha didn't want to go down. "Can the car get back up?" she said.

The Pension Ultimo had twelve rooms on two levels. The Señora Tarragona had her own apartment on the beach level where we were sitting now while she was talking.

"So Dr. Villanueva sent you?" she said. "He's always doing that. Even in the off season. He must know I am closed now, but he wants to remind me."

"Remind you of what?"

"That he still has his guilt," she said. "He told you about the war, didn't he? He calls it a catharsis therapy, but it is his obsession.

How far did he get?" she said. "Did he get to the part where they drove through Palma in the Lancia? And where they threw the bodies near the cemetery?"

"Yes."

"He is going through his phase of morbid melancholia again," the Señora Tarragona said. "He speaks of that time as the moral insanity of the world." The señora touched her pointed chin with her long fingers and looked at us to see if we were worthy. "He was part of it you know," she said. "He was in that Lancia too. He will tell you that later. He will tell you all about the prison ships with the search lights on them at night. That was my home during the war," she said. "That's why he sends me customers now. This obsessive guilt, then morbid melancholia. It would have been easier for him if his side had lost. Then he could have been punished. But his side won and nobody punished him. Even after the Second World War he expected the Americans to land and to punish him. When you called on him about your wife he must have thought you had come for this reason. You disappointed him," she said. "And because no one has punished him he has decided to punish himself. The next time you see him he will tell you the part he played. He is working up to his catharsis. He is about to punish himself again. Moral insanity is his favorite word when he enters his phase of morbid melancholia."

"You must have studied medicine," I said.

"Before the war, before Dr. Villanueva's moral insanity, I was a doctor too," she said.

Señora Tarragona had a long, dusty, olive face with huge eyes under too delicate eyebrows that swept back and gave her a kind of tragi-comic look. She sat stiffly and delicately as though fragile and a sudden movement would break her.

"That is why he sends me customers," she said. "Because he can no longer send me patients."

I gathered that Dr. Villaneuva had ruined her, destroyed her as a doctor when he was powerful, his moral insanity, but I did not want to push it and I changed the subject.

"Is there some place else you can recommend?" I said.

"This side of the island is no good," she said. "There are prevailing winds here all winter. Why don't you go to Madrid and see the Prado?"

"Martha would like to get some sketching in and I thought I would work here a while," I said. "Get some writing done."

"Before you can write," she said, "you should have something to write about. Go to Madrid and see the Prado. And do not be overwhelmed by Goya," she said to Martha, placing a long finger at her temple and staring at us intently. "Goya always overwhelms everyone at first. You have to learn to live with Goya. Ten, twenty years and then he does not overwhelm you and you can appreciate Goya. You can always appreciate El Greco. Velasquez takes more work, but he is worth it. When you come back to Goya, when he no longer overwhelms you, then you can appreciate his subtleties, his tremendous color, his impeccable sense of form and organization. You can shorten this period somewhat," she said, "by turning a Goya upside down."

When we left the Señora Tarragona's pension the Seat 600 made it up the cliff okay that Martha had been concerned about.

"It doesn't have much power, but it has four gears," I said as we made our way toward Puerta de Soller for lunch. To get to Puerta de Soller you have to drive inland again and go back through the Monasterio Lluch and Fornalutx, through incredibly steep splendid mountains and switchbacks where you have to come to a dead stop and you can see all the way to Ibiza. Puerta de Soller is another natural harbor that the sea has cut out of the rocks. It is about two miles wide, a dark, deep, indigo blue all the way from Sa Calobra where the lighthouse is, over to the esplanade where we sat in a broad outdoor sidewalk café after Martha got some Bisontes from a corner *kiosca* shaped like a castle. Martha asked the waiter for the *mapa*. After she had asked the gas station attendant for a *carta* to tell the roads it was natural that she should ask the waiter for a *mapa* to tell the foods, but he brought her a *carta* anyway.

"You're wrong," she said to me. "They speak Spanish here and they brought me the menu."

"They speak Mallorquin here," I said, "and they bring everybody the menu."

We had the *turistica*, a *prix-fixe* lunch whose price is controlled by the government depending on the category. This category was 1B and it cost fifty-five *pesetas*, about a dollar, *vino de la casa* included. The Mallorquins are loyal about their wine, but I find it a little rough, a surprisingly aggressive wine to be cultivated and encouraged by people who are so gentle.

"That's an Italian ship in the harbor," I said, looking out and noticing the flag. "So Dr. Villanueva's Italians have returned."

"But this time," Martha said, looking up from her *mapa*, "without the moral insanity."

I noticed now there were Italian sailors sitting around the café. They were being treated like anyone else.

"People don't forgive," I said, "but they forget because they have to forget, because it's too painful to remember."

"Not Dr. Villanueva," she said.

"He's a special case," I said. "Not only that he did more but that he should have known better."

"He's the only one who wants to talk about it."

"Maybe he's the only one who has to," I said.

I tried out my Italian on a sailor who was sitting alongside us. We had crossed on an Italian ship, the *Leonardo da Vinci*, and had worked at learning Italian. I asked him how he liked it here. He said the food was not bad but he found the wine a little sharp. Then he added as an afterthought, the people are a little strange. Then his comrade broke in with, "I don't like the way they look at us. You'd think we were criminals."

"Yes," the first Italian sailor said. "You'd think we had done something wrong." Then he leaned his head back in recollection, but he could think of nothing, and then he said quickly, as though recalling, "We helped them during their war. What more do they want? That is, I believe we did. I am too young to remember."

"That's right," the other sailor said. "We are all too young."

Then the first sailor took a drink of his wine and set down the glass carefully. He had a short, close-cut beard and a face that was dark, as dark as a Spaniard's. "All I can remember," he said carefully and in genuine thought, "Is that in their war we helped them. If it went wrong it must have been their doing."

"Remember," the other sailor said, "when it happened we were not born."

They got up now to go back to their freighter that was leaving. They left a ten *peseta* tip on the table and when the Italians left the waiter handed the tip back to them.

"And we were not born," the bearded Italian protested spreading his hands palm up to me before they turned for the ship. "We were not born."

We wanted to get back to Palma before it got dark so we cut over to Inca, a flat road down the center of Mallorca that would avoid the mountains. It went by an endless phalanx of huge robot windmills out of Cervantes that must have been here before anyone was born, ever.

In Palma we had dinner inside at the Formentor. We had the *langostas a la parilla* with a Spanish wine from Andalucia which cost only a few *pesetas* more than the local. Then we had *café-solo*, the best coffee in the world, before we went back to the Londres.

At the Londres the desk clerk said that Dr. Villaneuva had called three times and I was to call him at this number. I told the clerk it would not be necessary but he kept holding out the piece of paper as though I did not understand. I took it to relieve him and we climbed the three more flights up to get to our room. You already had to climb up one flight to get to the lobby. When I took the room I told the clerk that three flights would kill Martha and he told me that the lobby floor was reserved for people who took the full *pension*. He said if we took the full *pension mi esposa* would not be killed. I said the food on the full *pension* would probably kill her too and she preferred to die climbing because the Formentor just outside was probably the best restaurant in Spain and that is the best way to die.

"They're always talking about me dying," Martha said as we climbed all the way up and put our coats on the big delicate brass bed. "I'll be all right as soon as I get over what I caught in Casablanca. Dr. Villanueva said there was nothing more he could do for me, that it would just take a little time."

"I don't think we'll be seeing Dr. Villanueva any more," I said.

"I don't think we will either," she said.

Dr. Villanueva called very early in the morning, at about six o'clock and I refused to take the call. At nine we went out for breakfast at the Formentor. In the lobby the clerk asked me if I had learned about Dr. Villanueva. I said, no, I was not interested. When we started down the final marble flight of stairs the clerk hollered after me, "He did it with a small Italian pistol, a Biretta. Dr. Villanueva *es muerto*. Dr. Villanueva is dead," the clerk said.

JACK ARMSTRONG IN TANGIER is published in an
edition of 500. Of 175 hardbound copies offered for sale
50 have been signed by the author. There are 300 copies
in paper wrappers.